Taking Off

A Maryellen Classic
Volume 2

by Valerie Tripp

✴American Girl®

Questions or comments? Call 1-800-845-0005,
visit **americangirl.com**, or write to Customer Service,
American Girl, 8400 Fairway Place, Middleton, WI 53562.

15 16 17 18 19 20 21 LEO 10 9 8 7 6 5 4 3 2 1

Cover image by Michael Dwornik and Juliana Kolesova

Cataloging-in-Publication Data available from the Library of Congress

For Elizabeth Jane

Beforever™

The adventurous characters you'll meet in
the BeForever books will spark your curiosity
about the past, inspire you to find your voice
in the present, and excite you about your future.
You'll make friends with these girls as you share
their fun and their challenges. Like you, they are
bright and brave, imaginative and energetic,
creative and kind. Just as you are, they are
discovering what really matters: Helping others.
Being a true friend. Protecting the earth.
Standing up for what's right. Read their stories,
explore their worlds, join their adventures.
Your friendship with them will BeForever.

✳ TABLE *of* CONTENTS ✳

❄✳❄✳❄✳❄

Bridesmaids, Birthdays, and Brainstorms

✻ CHAPTER ONE ✻

en!" Maryellen Larkin exclaimed happily. "On my birthday, I'll be ten."

Maryellen and her friends were walking home from school on a sunny April afternoon. Exuberantly, Maryellen sprang ahead of the other girls and then spun around to face them. "My birthday is Saturday, May seventh, which is coming soon, in just three weeks and a little bit." Maryellen skipped backward, bouncing on her toes. "Oh boy! I've been waiting to be ten my *whole life.*"

"Me, too," said her friends, Karen King, Karen Stohlman, and Angela Terlizzi.

"What kind of party are you going to have, Ellie?" asked Karen King, getting down to serious business. "Bowling?"

"No, I did that last year," said Maryellen. "And the

year before that, miniature golf, and the year before *that*, a beach party. I want to do something new, something that no one's ever done before."

"I know!" said Karen Stohlman. "You could have your party at the drive-in movie!"

"And eat cake and ice cream in the car?" said Maryellen. "And open *presents* in the car? That won't work."

"How about a Davy Crockett party? We'll wear our coonskin caps," said Karen King. *Davy Crockett* was everyone's favorite television show. It was about an American hero, Davy Crockett, who lived in the wild mountains of Tennessee in the eighteen hundreds. All the kids had hats with long fur tails like the one Davy Crockett wore. Maryellen even had "Daisy Crockett" underwear with a female version of Davy on it. "Maybe your mom could make your birthday cake in the shape of a coonskin cap," Karen King continued. "And we could all sing the TV show theme song." Karen sang out loud and clear: "*Davy, Davy Crockett, king of the wild frontier!*"

"No," said Angela. "We'll sing, '*Ellie, Ellie Larkin, queen of Day-to-na Beach!*'"

This struck all four girls as hilariously funny, and they laughed hard until Karen King brought them down to earth by asking, "Speaking of Davy, will you invite Davy Fenstermacher to your party this year? You have every other year."

"That was back when we were friends," said Maryellen. Davy Fenstermacher lived next door to the Larkins. He and Maryellen used to be best friends. They'd ride their bikes to school together, eat lunch together, and play together after school and on weekends. But they'd had a falling-out back at the beginning of the school year, and their friendship still was not repaired. Davy never even spoke to Maryellen anymore.

"Davy wouldn't come to my party if I asked him, now," she said. "He's too busy being best friends with Wayne."

"Wayne the Pain," said Karen Stohlman.

Maryellen said briskly, "Ten is too old to have boys at your birthday party anyway. You don't have boys again until you're teenagers in high school, and the boys are your boyfriends, and you play records and dance, sort of like a sock hop only at your house."

The girls were silent for a moment. They knew what a sock hop was: It was a dance where you took off your shoes and danced in your socks so that you wouldn't scuff up the floor. They were trying to imagine even *wanting* to do such a thing as dance with a boy, especially one like Wayne, who, they felt certain, would only be *more* Wayne-ish and pain-ish in high school than he was now.

"Joan told me about high school parties," Maryellen added. "That's how I know."

"Ah!" said the girls. They were in awe of Joan, Maryellen's eldest sister, who was eighteen. They respected Joan as their highest authority on fashion, romance, and being grown-up. After all, Joan was engaged to her boyfriend, Jerry, who had been a sailor in the Korean War and was now in college. Joan and Jerry were already planning their wedding, which was to take place at the end of the summer. Maryellen was thrilled, because she was going to be a bridesmaid.

Suddenly, she stopped short. "Oh!" she gasped. "I've just had a brilliant idea."

"What?" cried Angela, Karen, and Karen. "What's your idea? Tell us!"

Maryellen held up her hands, palms straight, to stop her friends from talking. "What if," she began dramatically, "I have a movie-star birthday party and everyone comes dressed as her favorite movie star? I'll be Debbie Reynolds and wear my bridesmaid dress."

"Oh, I love that idea!" said Karen King.

"A movie-star party!" said Karen Stohlman. "Neato! No one has ever done *that* before!"

The girls started naming all the most glamorous movie stars of 1955.

"I'll be Audrey Hepburn," said Angela.

"Dibs on Grace Kelly," said Karen Stohlman.

"I can't decide if I want to be Elizabeth Taylor or Marilyn Monroe," sighed Karen King. "Or maybe I'll be a television star like Lucille Ball from *I Love Lucy*."

"Scooter could come as Rin Tin Tin or Lassie," joked Maryellen. "I'll be J. Fred Muggs, the chimpanzee!" She loped along the sidewalk, swinging her arms as if she were the famous television star chimpanzee.

The girls laughed themselves breathless, and then Maryellen said, "Now I'm even more excited about my birthday!"

"Me, too," said Karen Stohlman. "I can't wait to see

your bridesmaid dress. I bet it's gorgeous. What does it look like?"

"Well," said Maryellen. "It *will* be gorgeous, when it's finished. Mom's making it."

"Oh," said the girls. They hesitated for a teeny, tiny second. "Good."

Maryellen knew what her friends were thinking, because she was thinking the same thing, too. They'd all had unfortunate experiences with their mothers making dresses as part of do-it-yourself crazes. Maryellen knew that her friends were too polite to say so, but dresses made by mothers did not always turn out very well.

Angela was first to think of something optimistic to say. "Since your mom is making it, your dress will fit you perfectly," she said.

Maryellen grinned gratefully. "I certainly hope so," she said. "Or else the movie star I'll look like at my birthday party will be the scarecrow from *The Wizard of Oz*!"

✳

"Ellie, honey, stand still," said Mrs. Larkin.

Maryellen held her breath. She was standing on a chair while Mom, kneeling and frowning with concentration, was pinning the tissue-paper dress pattern onto her to see where it would need to be taken in. Maryellen was as skinny as a flagpole, so Mom was using lots of pins. Maryellen noticed that Mom also seemed to be sighing a lot. Even Maryellen's energetic imagination had to strain to imagine how a dress would emerge from the tissue-paper pattern. Pinned together, the paper pieces looked about as shapely as Scooter, the Larkins' pudgy dachshund. Maybe it had been a mistake to beg Mom to make her bridesmaid dress first. Mom was also going to make bridesmaid dresses for Carolyn, Maryellen's next oldest sister, who was fourteen, and Beverly, who was seven. *Maybe*, thought Maryellen, *I should have waited until Mom knew what she was doing, sewing-wise. Ah, well, too late now!* At least she hadn't told Mom yet that she was counting on having her dress finished by her birthday so that she could wear it to her movie-star birthday party. Adding the pressure of a deadline that was only a few weeks away would put Mom right over the top with nervousness, she could tell.

Mrs. Larkin sighed again, sounding harassed. Joan, the bride-to-be, looked up from the book that she was reading and said gently, "Mom? You don't have to do this, you know. I'd be just as happy with ready-made bridesmaid dresses bought off the rack from O'Neal's."

"No, no, no," said Mrs. Larkin. She sat back on her heels and dabbed her sweaty forehead with the back of her wrist. "No, I'm determined to make the dresses. Your dad and I were married during the Depression, and so I didn't have any bridesmaids at my wedding, and I was married in a suit—a borrowed suit at that! I want to do for you everything that I missed out on, Joanie."

"Jerry and I don't need a big fuss," said Joan. "Just a small wedding is fine with us."

"Nonsense," said Mrs. Larkin. "A girl's wedding day is the most important day in her life! Your father and I want yours to be perfect in every detail: your cake, your flowers, your veil . . ."

Maryellen piped up, "Your hair, your shoes . . ."

"Jerry and I have talked about getting married outdoors, in a garden or a park," said Joan. "So I'll probably wear flats. We don't want to be all stiff and uncomfortable."

"But I was hoping Jerry would wear his dress-whites Navy uniform!" said Mom.

"That's so formal," said Joan. "We want to be relaxed."

"Joan!" said Mom. "Flats? A park? This is your wedding, not a wienie roast. Honestly, sometimes I think I'm more excited about your marriage than you are." Mom took a pin and—*jab!*—used it to pin the paper pattern for the collar onto Maryellen's shoulder.

Maryellen suspected that the collar was backward. But she stayed quiet while Joan said, "Oh, no, no. I'm excited about the *marriage*. I'm thrilled to be marrying Jerry. But to me, marriage is one thing and the wedding is another. The marriage is forever and the wedding is only one day. And don't get me wrong; I'm grateful for all that you're doing. Jerry and I want our wedding to be beautiful, just not stuffy and fussy and such a big deal."

"It's not stuffy or fussy to do things correctly," said Mom. "I am determined that you and Jerry will have a proper wedding. For heaven's sake, you're such a bookworm that if I left it up to you, you'd probably get married on the steps of the public library."

"And carry books for a bouquet," joked Maryellen.

"Well, I do love books *almost* as much as I love Jerry," Joan said, smiling. "But I promise I won't get married at the library, Mom. I promise you can have my wedding your way."

Mom smiled, too. "So you're giving me permission to go full speed ahead?"

"Aye, aye, captain," said Joan with a laugh.

Maryellen was glad to see Mom laugh as well— even though laughing distracted her so that she pinned the paper pattern for the sash on backward, too.

✳

The next day at school, Maryellen's fourth-grade teacher, Mrs. Humphrey, wrote on the blackboard:

Today is Tuesday, April 12, 1955.

"Wayne Philpott," said Mrs. Humphrey without turning around, "if you shoot that rubber band at Maryellen, you and I will be having lunch together the rest of the week."

Davy snatched the rubber band away from Wayne

and put it in his desk, and Maryellen crossed her eyes
and stuck out her tongue at Wayne over her shoulder.
Sometimes she was glad that Mrs. Humphrey seemed
to have eyes in the back of her head!

"Boys and girls," said Mrs. Humphrey, facing the
class. "Give me your attention, please. Today we're
going to go to a special assembly for the whole school
in the auditorium."

Everyone wiggled and whispered, and Wayne
hooted, "Yahoo!"

"I know that my fourth-graders will act like ladies
and gentlemen," said Mrs. Humphrey.

Everyone looked at Wayne, who batted his eye-
lashes, folded his hands on his desk, and smiled
innocently.

"Line up, please," said Mrs. Humphrey.

All the students jumped up from their desks.
Wayne tried to trip Maryellen on her way to the girls'
line. Luckily, she heard someone—maybe it was
Davy—murmur "Watch it!" just in the nick of time, so
she hopped over Wayne's foot.

"Quiet in the hallway, please," said Mrs. Humphrey.

As Maryellen and her classmates filed into the

auditorium, she saw the principal, Mr. Carey, up front
fiddling with the dials on the television set. Mr. Carey's
eyeglasses were pushed up on his forehead. He was
squinting at the dials, and moving the rabbit-ears
antenna to get a clear picture on the television screen. It
seemed to be a news program. The screen was too little
and too far away for Maryellen or any other student
to see, really. Mr. Carey had the volume turned up
very loud, which only added to the cacophony in the
noisy auditorium as students chatted, squeaked their
seats, shuffled their feet, and called and waved to their
friends in other classes.

Mr. Carey flicked the lights on and off for quiet,
and then held his pointer finger up to his lips. "*Shhh!*"
he shushed. Finally, he just bellowed, "QUIET!"

As everyone hushed, Angela whispered to
Maryellen, "Do you think we're here to get good news
or bad news?"

"Good news," said Maryellen, who always liked to
hope for the best.

"Ten years ago today, President Franklin Delano
Roosevelt died," said the TV newscaster. "Roosevelt
could not walk, because he had had polio, a terrible

disease that has killed many people, especially children. Three years ago, in 1952, a polio epidemic affected over fifty thousand people in the United States, and killed nearly three thousand. But today, Dr. Jonas Salk, at the University of Pittsburgh, announced that he has found a safe and effective vaccine to prevent polio. The whole world is grateful to Dr. Salk, and to the more than one hundred million Americans who contributed money to research for polio prevention. And now, the task before us is to raise public awareness and to raise money to produce and distribute the vaccine."

The TV newscaster went on, but no one heard the rest of the announcement, because the auditorium exploded with cheers. The students jumped up and down and clapped and whistled while the teachers hugged one another and cried happy tears. A way to prevent polio was very good news indeed. Outside, Maryellen heard church bells ringing and sirens going off in celebration.

She felt someone poke her in the back. It was Davy. He grinned and raised his eyebrows. Then he turned away without saying anything, but that didn't matter. Maryellen knew that Davy's grin was a tiny, silent, split-second celebration just between the two of them. Davy was letting her know that he realized how the news about the polio vaccine meant even more to her than it did to most people, because when she was younger, she had had polio. She was all better now. Really, the only reminder was that one leg was a tiny bit weaker than the other, and her lungs were extra sensitive to cold.

But Maryellen remembered very well how much polio had hurt. Sometimes in her dreams she had polio again, and the heavy, dark, frightened feeling of being lost in pain and worry came back. With all her heart, she was glad that now, due to Dr. Salk, no one else— neither her friends, nor her sisters or brothers, nor children she'd never met—would ever have to know that terrible feeling. And she was glad that even though Davy didn't seem to want to be her friend anymore, he understood how she felt.

"Well, I can't say that I'm looking forward to getting a shot," said Karen Stohlman as the girls filed out of the auditorium. "I hate shots." She turned to Maryellen and said, "You're a lucky duck, Ellie. You won't have to get a shot because you already had polio."

Maryellen didn't exactly think she was a lucky duck. First of all, she wasn't lucky at all to have had a terrible illness like polio. Second, she actually felt sort of left out because she wouldn't be getting a shot like everybody else. She wanted to be part of something important and historic, something that was going to change the world for the better.

"I won't be getting a shot, either," said Carol Turner, another girl in their class. "My mother says vaccinations are dangerous." Carol shivered. "You know, when you get a vaccination, they're putting a dead virus in you."

"Eww!" said Karen King. "I don't want anybody to put viruses in me, dead or alive. Now I'm scared to get a shot!"

"Are you kidding?" Maryellen asked in horrified disbelief. "Finally there's a shot to protect you from a really terrible disease, a disease that can cripple you or even kill you, and you're afraid to get it?"

Carol Turner shrugged. "I bet a lot of people think the vaccine is dangerous like my mom does, so they won't get a shot."

"But—but—" Maryellen sputtered, stunned speechless with outrage. Just then, she had a brainstorm. She stopped still right in the middle of the hallway and announced to her friends, "I've decided about my birthday party."

"It's a movie-star party, right?" said Karen Stohlman.

"No," said Maryellen. A movie-star party seemed self-indulgent and frivolous now. She had thought of a way that her birthday could Do Something Important. "We're going to put on a show. And the point of the show will be to encourage people to get a polio shot. We'll charge ten cents admission, and send the money to the March of Dimes to help pay for the polio vaccine for poor children."

Angela hopped and clapped her hands in glee. "And I thought the movie-star idea was good!" she said. "A show is much better!"

Maryellen agreed. She was excited, pleased, and proud that she had thought of a way to help Dr. Salk fight polio. And she felt certain that she could figure out a way to wear her bridesmaid dress in her show, too.

Rock Around the Clock

* CHAPTER TWO *

his was it! Maryellen was so excited that her heart felt fluttery. Today was the day of the first rehearsal of her show.

All the performers—the two Karens and Angela, plus Maryellen's sisters Carolyn and Beverly—were sitting on the driveway facing the carport, just the way the audience would be for the real show. Maryellen's two little brothers, Tom and Mikey, were sitting on the driveway, too, with Scooter between them. The boys had begged and begged to be in "Maryellen's Dr. Salt show," which Tom kept on saying no matter how many times she told him the name was Salk, not Salt. Finally, Mom said that she should let the boys be in the show and keep them out of Mom's hair while she sewed. So Maryellen gave in. She wanted to encourage Mom to sew because the deadline for her bridesmaid dress was drawing nearer and nearer.

"Look, everybody!" Maryellen sang out. "I made posters to advertise our show." She held up two of her posters. One showed the heads and shoulders of rows and rows of smiling children and the other showed a giant dime. On the posters, Maryellen had printed, "Stop polio! Get a shot!" Across the bottom, she'd written, "You can help. Come to a show at the Larkins' house on Saturday, May 7, at 3 p.m. 10 cents admission to be donated to the March of Dimes."

"Ooooh," everyone murmured appreciatively.

"The posters are swell," said Karen King.

"I made three of each kind," said Maryellen proudly.

"Great!" said Carolyn. "We'll put them up all around the neighborhood."

"Ellie, you are such a good artist!" added Angela. "You're as good as Grandma Moses."

"Thank you," said Maryellen, pleased to be compared to one of the most famous artists of 1955. "Now, pretend there are sheets hanging behind me like theater curtains, hiding the garage part of the carport so that it's backstage."

"Okay," giggled the girls.

Maryellen went on, "I'll read the script out loud, and you can each decide what part you want to play."

"Hurray!" everyone cheered in happy anticipation.

Before Maryellen had read one word, Davy and Wayne appeared from next door. Davy was being pushed from behind by his mother, who had her hands on his shoulders to propel him forward. "Davy wants to be in your little show, Ellie, sweetie," said Mrs. Fenstermacher. "Your mother told me about it when she called for some sewing advice, and I thought it was the cutest idea. Just *darling*. And I said, 'Davy, you are going to be in Ellie's adorable birthday-party polio show.' He's shy, but he really wants to. Don't you, hon?"

"I guess so," said Davy, with about as much enthusiasm as he'd have for eating a bowl of worms. Maryellen knew he never would have come over on his own.

"Uh, all right," she said. She didn't mind Davy being in the show. In fact, she was glad—except that Wayne would tag along as always.

Mrs. Fenstermacher went inside to give Mrs. Larkin her sewing scissors, and Wayne flung himself onto the driveway. He smirked up at Maryellen, making it clear that he was not going anywhere. As usual, Wayne was wearing his propeller beanie hat. And as usual, she wished the propeller would lift Wayne up like a helicopter and carry him far, far away.

Maryellen ignored Wayne and began to read the script she had written. "Fighting Polio. Act One. In Dr. Jonas Salk's laboratory."

Maryellen was so proud of her script that she could practically burst! Her show was a musical. She had written different words to tunes that everyone knew, inspired by the way Angela had changed the words to the *Davy Crockett* theme song. For example, to the tune of "There Was a Farmer Had a Dog, and Bingo Was His Name-o," she had written:

> *There was a very bad disease*
> *And polio was its name-o,*
> *P-O-L-I-O, P-O-L-I-O, P-O-L-I-O*
> *And polio was its name-o.*

That song was in the first act, which was about polio and Dr. Salk discovering the vaccine. The second act was all about encouraging people to get a polio vaccine shot. To the tune of "Old MacDonald Had a Farm," Maryellen had written:

> *Get a shot so you won't catch*
> *Poh-lee, oh-lee, oh!*

In both acts, the narrator did all the talking while actors silently acted out what the narrator was saying. Maryellen was planning to be the narrator herself, of course, so that she could wear her bridesmaid dress.

As she read her script aloud, she couldn't help noticing that everyone's enthusiasm was fading. Before she had finished reading the first act, Karen King was playing jacks with Beverly, Carolyn and Angela were comparing toenail polish, Wayne was putting grass on Karen Stohlman's hair, and Tom and Mikey looked dazed and glazed. It was impossible to tell how Davy felt because he was lying with his head on Scooter's back, looking up at the clouds. But Maryellen plowed on, believing that every word she had written was essential. When she finally said, "The End," everyone clapped halfheartedly. Only Wayne clapped hard.

"I'm clapping because I'm so relieved that it's finally over!" Wayne said. "For cryin' out loud! Listening to that show is about as much fun as getting a shot for poh-lee, oh-lee, oh."

"No comments from the peanut gallery, Wayne," said Carolyn. She turned to Maryellen and said kindly, "The show feels too long, but I think it's just that the driveway is too hard to sit on. And scorching hot. People will need pillows or beach chairs or something."

"Okay," said Maryellen.

"Well, no offense, Ellie," said Karen King, who was not afraid to be blunt, "but I think the play feels too long because it *is* too long. It needs to be shorter or funnier or something, or people won't like it."

"I guess I could make it a bit shorter," said Maryellen, trying to be a good sport. No one seemed to appreciate how hard she had worked, writing the play all by herself, with no help from anybody. Gosh, sometimes she'd crept silently into the bathroom in the middle of the night, sat cross-legged on the floor, opened her notebook, and by the pale glow of the night-light, written and rewritten pages and pages. Now, reluctantly, she said, "I guess I could cut out some of the songs."

"No, don't cut the songs," said Beverly. "They're the only good parts."

"But the music is sort of babyish," said Carolyn, who'd recently gone crazy for rock 'n' roll. "People like hit tunes like 'Rock Around the Clock.'"

"Better music might help," said Karen King, speaking to Carolyn as if Maryellen were invisible. "But the way the narrator drones on and on and on is boring."

"Maybe the show just needs more variety," said Angela.

"In fact, a variety show would be better all the way around, if you ask me," said Wayne.

"No one did ask you," said Maryellen crossly. "Mind your own beeswax."

But while Maryellen was scolding Wayne, Karen Stohlman was saying enthusiastically, "Variety—that's it! Let's put on a variety show, like *The Ed Sullivan Show* on TV. We can each do different acts, like singing and dancing and juggling and magic tricks."

"That would be more fun for the audience," said Carolyn.

"And for us, too," said Karen King, "because we'll each get to do what we *like* to do and show off our talents, instead of just being silent dummies with nothing to say for ourselves."

"Wait," Maryellen said. She felt as if her show was galloping away from her, out of her control. "I—"

But Karen Stohlman rose to her toes and did a pirouette as she went on, "Beverly and I can do ballet."

"I'll play rock 'n' roll on the piano!" offered Carolyn.

"Angela and I can dance and sing," said Karen King. And to prove it, she and Angela started to jitterbug and sing,

> We're gonna rock around the clock tonight,
> We're gonna rock, rock, rock
> Till broad daylight,
> We're gonna rock, we're gonna rock
> Around the clock tonight.

"You can do rope tricks," Wayne suggested to Davy, "and lasso Scooter!"

Even Tom piped up, "Mikey and I can do a puppet show with our Howdy Doody puppets."

"What'll I do?" asked Maryellen. No one heard her, so she said again loudly, "What'll I do?"

Everyone was quiet for a moment, trying hard to think of what Maryellen's talent might be.

"You already made those great posters," said Carolyn at last.

"But what'll I do in the *show*?" asked Maryellen.

Davy sat up. "You're good at talking," he said. "Tell jokes or something."

"Like, why did the clown throw the clock out the window?" said Wayne. "Because he wanted to see time fly. Get it?"

"Be quiet, Mr. Helicopter Head," said Maryellen. "I don't want to tell silly jokes. I want to encourage people to get vaccinated, which is serious and important."

"Well, then make a short speech about Jonas Salk," said Carolyn, "and sing one of your songs. Maybe the one about getting vaccinated, the 'poh-lee, oh-lee, oh' song."

"Yes, that would be good!" said Angela brightly.

Maryellen hugged her script close to her chest. All that hard work for nothing! She was sorely disappointed. But it was clear that no one wanted to do the show that she had written. They just wanted to sing and dance and show off. She had no choice; she couldn't do her show all by herself! So she gave in.

"All right," she said. At least she'd get to wear her bridesmaid dress—if Mom had finished it. *That might be a big if,* Maryellen thought. *I'd better ask Mom how my dress is coming along.*

✳

That evening, Carolyn was at a sock hop at the high school gym, and Maryellen and Scooter rode along in the car when Mom went to pick up Carolyn after the dance. It was unusual to have Mom all to herself, and Maryellen knew that she should ask about the bridesmaid dress, but she wasn't quite sure how to begin. She was still hesitant about bugging Mom. Finally, she said, "Gosh! Carolyn has changed, hasn't she? She never would have gone to a sock hop last year. Next thing you know, she'll be going to the prom in a prom dress, with a corsage and a boyfriend and everything, like Joan."

"Carolyn's a real teenager now," agreed Mom. "She's what the magazines call a 'bobby-soxer.'" Mom smiled, and then said with a sigh, "All you kids are growing up so fast! It feels like just a minute ago Joan got her first prom dress. Remember that gorgeous pink one? It's still in the closet somewhere. And now Joan's getting *married*, for goodness sakes."

Maryellen grabbed her chance. "By the way," she asked casually, "how's my bridesmaid dress coming along?"

"Well, Mrs. Fenstermacher helped me cut the fabric," said Mom. "Now I just have to sew the pieces together."

That didn't sound too hard. "Do you think, I mean, I was wondering if you might have it finished by my birthday?" Maryellen asked.

"Ellie, sweetie," Mom said, sounding tense. "When you're planning a wedding, a lot has to be done far in advance. So even though the wedding is not until the end of the summer, I'm already awfully busy with the preparations. There's so much to do, and I want it all to be perfect. I've got to reserve the caterer and decide the menu. Then I've got to order flowers from the florist, and find musicians and choose the music . . . The list goes on and on. I don't know if I'll have time to finish your dress by next week or not. We'll see."

Scooter snorted in his sleep, as if to say, *Humpf—* *"we'll see" isn't very reassuring.*

That was what Maryellen was thinking, too.

Mom seemed glad to change the subject as they pulled up to the high school. "Run in and tell Carolyn we're here, please, sweetheart," she said to Maryellen.

As Maryellen walked in, rock 'n' roll music was blaring so loudly that the whole gym seemed to be thumping to the beat. The gym was packed with girls in pretty, swirly dresses and boys in letter sweaters or jackets and ties, and it was decorated with loops of colorful crepe paper strung between the basketball hoops and the windows. All along the walls, shoes were lined up, and the kids on the dance floor were in their socks, dancing fast to rock 'n' roll. Maryellen thought the sock hop *did* sort of look like fun, except for the dancing-with-a-boy part. She looked around, and when she spotted Carolyn, she hardly recognized her. Carolyn was dancing with a boy, dancing as well as a dancer on TV! And she looked beautiful. At home, Carolyn wore the bobby-soxer's standard outfit of jeans with the cuffs rolled up, an old shirt of Dad's tied at the waist, bobby socks, and penny loafers. But tonight she was fancy. The full skirt of her dress was nipped in at the waist, and it swooshed gracefully when her partner twirled her under his arm. Her feet just *flew*. Maryellen caught Carolyn's eye and waved. Carolyn waved back, and as the music ended, she said good-bye to her partner and hurried over.

As she watched Carolyn come toward her, waving good-bye to her friends, her eyes sparkling and her cheeks flushed, Maryellen had a quick, jumbled-up mix of feelings. She felt a little envy, a little pride, a little sorrow, a little curiosity, and underneath it all, hope for her own future. Being a teenager looked pretty nice.

✳

Hope was something that Maryellen needed more and more as rehearsals for the birthday-party variety show went on. Every day after school, everyone in the show came over to the Larkins' house to practice. At least they were supposed to be practicing. But really Wayne and Davy just ran around lassoing each other, chased by Tom and Mikey. The ballerinas, Beverly and Karen Stohlman, couldn't agree on who'd do what in their ballet. Carolyn was always inside talking on the hall phone with a boy named Douglas Newswander, who was the one she'd danced with at the sock hop.

And Karen King kept changing her mind about what song she and Angela would sing.

"Oh, I've had the most wonderful idea," Karen King said to Angela the afternoon before the show was supposed to go on. "Instead of singing 'Rock Around the Clock,' let's sing 'How Much Is That Doggie in the Window?' We can borrow poodle skirts from Ellie and Karen Stohlman, and Scooter can be the doggie in the window! Won't that be cute?"

"Mm-hmm," said Angela. "Except I don't know the words to that song."

"I do," said Karen King. "It goes like this:

> *How much is that doggie in the window?*
> *Something, something, waggedy tail.*
> *How much is that doggie in the window?*
> *La la la la doggie's for sale.*

"Anyway, sort of like that," Karen King went on breezily. "It'll be easy to learn the words."

"By tomorrow?" asked Maryellen, trying not to sound shrill. "You're going to learn the something, somethings and la la la's by tomorrow? Because that's when the show is. It's way too late to be loosey-goosey. This is our last rehearsal."

"We know," said Karen King with exaggerated calmness. "You don't have to get all huffy about it."

"Also," said Maryellen, "good luck talking Scooter into having a 'waggedy tail' or doing anything you want him to do when you want him to do it." Davy had already given up on lassoing Scooter because Scooter wouldn't sit up. Scooter would just lie there looking like a sack of potatoes. "Davy has to lasso me instead of Scooter," she pointed out.

"Well, if you're going to be Scooter for Davy, you can be a doggie in the window for Karen and me, if Scooter won't cooperate," said Angela. "You could tie Davy's rope around your waist, and swing the end to be the waggedy tail."

"Ohhh-kay," said Maryellen tepidly. Her own part in the show was so small that she was filling in anyplace, in any act, where anyone needed her for anything. For example, neither Beverly nor Karen Stohlman wanted to be the boy ballerina in their ballet because they both wanted to wear a tutu. So Maryellen had to wear pants and be the one they leaned on when they stood on tiptoe. She also had to help Tom and Mikey with their puppet show. Tom and Mikey liked to move the puppets, but they didn't know what to say, so Maryellen had to make up a story for them to match what the puppets were doing, which was mostly sleeping, waking up, and hugging, because that's really all Tom and Mikey knew how to make the puppets do. It was her job to turn the pages of Carolyn's sheet music because Carolyn hadn't yet memorized all the notes in the rock 'n' roll song she was going to play, called "Shake, Rattle and Roll."

Shaken, rattled, and not at all ready to roll was how Maryellen felt right now. It was time to rehearse the most important part of the show—her own speech and song. She stood in front of the carport and began. "Fighting Polio," she said, sort of out of breath. "Dr. Jonas Salk—"

"Wait a minute, Ellie," Karen King interrupted. "In the real show tomorrow, aren't you supposed to wear your bridesmaid dress when you make your speech? When'll you have time to change out of your pants?"

Maryellen pushed her hair off her sweaty forehead. "I guess after Carolyn's music." She didn't want to admit to herself or to anyone else that even though Mrs. Fenstermacher was over all the time helping Mom, her dress still wasn't finished.

There was another thing she didn't want to admit, either. And it was that her act, which was supposed to be the whole point of the show, was a dud. Her song wasn't too bad, but she had become accustomed to seeing people wander off when she practiced her earnest speech. Even Scooter sometimes left, and he never moved unless it was absolutely necessary or food was being offered. Once, in an effort to cheer her up, good old Carolyn had said, "Look on the bright side, Ellie. Your act will make people appreciate all the *other* acts more!" But Maryellen didn't feel cheered; she felt worried.

"Fighting Polio," Maryellen began again. She was surprised and gratified that this time, as she was making her speech and singing her song, everyone was watching for a change. They were even nodding and smiling. They seemed to be really enjoying her act. *Maybe I'm getting better at it*, she thought. *Or maybe they're just finally beginning to appreciate the important things I'm saying.*

Then, out of the corner of her eye, Maryellen caught a movement. She whirled around and found Wayne right behind her. He'd turned his eyeglasses upside down and made his hair stick out all over his head so that he looked like a mad scientist from a science-fiction comic book. He had helped himself to two test tubes from her chemistry set, which Mom allowed her to use only in the carport because of the rotten-egg smells the chemicals made. Wayne had squirted water from his squirt gun into one test tube and then poured the water from that test tube into another, as if he were Dr. Salk inventing the polio vaccine. With a sinking heart and a flash of indignation, Maryellen realized that Wayne had been behind her hamming it up the whole time, pretending to be Jonas Salk and miming the actions she'd described Dr. Salk doing in her speech.

As Maryellen watched, speechless, Wayne began shooting his squirt gun straight up in the air so that water flew up like a fountain as he sang,

> *Get a shot so you won't catch*
> *Poh-lee, oh-lee, oh!*

"Cut it out, Wayne!" Maryellen ordered. But her voice was lost in the claps and cheers of the other kids.

"Wayne, that was hilarious!" said Karen Stohlman. "You should do that in the real show tomorrow."

"Yes!" said Karen King. "It's a riot! The audience will love it."

"No!" exploded Maryellen. "I don't even want Wayne to come to the show, much less to be in it and ruin my act by making fun of it."

"Oh, come on, Ellie," coaxed Angela. "Wayne's funny."

"It's my show and my act and my idea and my party and my birthday," Maryellen said furiously, "so I get to say if Wayne can be in it or not. And I say, he *cannot*. And that's final."

Everyone was stunned into silence. Even Wayne had nothing to say. An odd expression crossed his face as he replaced the test tubes, and Maryellen realized that she'd hurt Wayne's feelings. *Good!* she thought. *Now he sees how it feels.*

"Listen, Ellie, people aren't puppets," said Karen King. "You can't just boss us around and make us do what you want us to do."

"All right then," said Maryellen. She was fed up.

"Do what you want. And I will do what I want. I quit."

"But you can't quit," wailed Carolyn. "It's *your* party."

"We can't do the show without you," said Davy.

Maryellen shrugged. "You should have thought of that before," she said. "It's too late now." And she flounced off into the house, slamming the screen door behind her.

Show Biz

A t dinner that evening, the family sat in the breakfast nook. Carolyn and Beverly squeezed themselves into the corner of the nook that was farthest away from Maryellen and would not look at her or speak to her. Tom and Mikey sneaked sideways glances at her as if they were afraid she was still the fierce sourpuss she'd been that afternoon at rehearsal.

Maryellen just toyed with her food. The minute dinner was over, she went outside, even though Mom had set up tray tables in the living room so that everyone could have dessert in front of the TV while they watched *The Lone Ranger*. Hearing her brothers and sisters all shout "Hi-yo, Silver!" along with the Lone Ranger as he called out to his horse made Maryellen feel as lone as the Ranger—and lonely and lonesome, too.

So she was glad when, after a little while, Dad and Scooter came outside. "Hi, sport," Dad said to her. "Want to help Scooter and me wash the car?"

"Yes!" said Maryellen. She loved getting the car—and herself—wet and sudsy. Dad handed her a bucket and a sponge, and she went to work washing the taillights. They were her favorite parts of the station wagon to wash because they reminded her of giant eyes, and the big tail fins reminded her of enormous, arching silver eyebrows.

"Rather a chilly atmosphere at dinner tonight, I thought," said Dad as he untangled the hose. "What's going on?"

"I had a big fight with everybody at rehearsal today," Maryellen said, "and I quit the show. Since it's my show, they can't really do it without me, so the whole thing is off."

"Hmm," said Dad. "That's too bad. I guess that means that your birthday party is off, too."

"Yes!" said Maryellen, indignant. "It's so unfair. It's *terrible*. I'm getting cheated out of my party, and none of it was my fault. Wayne ruined everything. I wanted the show to say something serious and important about polio, and he just made fun of it." She sighed. "I guess maybe it was a silly idea, anyway. I mean that my show could really do any good."

Dad squirted the car with the hose for a minute or two, and then he said, "You know, your show sort of reminds me of our bomb shelter."

"It does?" asked Maryellen. She wrung out her soapy sponge so that the water fell on her flip-flops to cool off her feet. "How?" She knew that bomb shelters were places for people to go to in case an atomic bomb fell. At school, there was no bomb shelter, so during air-raid drills, the students sat under their desks or crouched in the hallways with their arms crossed over their heads. At home, Dad had made a bomb shelter in a dug-out area underneath their house. Sometimes, she and Beverly played in the bomb shelter. Dad didn't mind as long as they didn't drink up the water, eat up the food, or use up the batteries in the flashlights he'd put there in case of emergency. Maryellen couldn't see how the bomb shelter was like her polio show at all.

"If an atomic bomb fell on Daytona Beach, it would wipe out everything here," said Dad. He nodded toward the bomb shelter as he swooshed a rag in the bucket of soapy water. "Our bomb shelter would probably be useless. But it's the most I can do to try to protect us. It's *all* I can do, so it's worth my effort. And your polio show is worth *your* effort, Ellie, because even if it isn't much, it's something that you can do. Something is always better than nothing. Trying is always better than giving up, right?"

"So you think I shouldn't cancel the show?" said Maryellen. "Is that what you're saying?"

"Not exactly," said Dad, wringing out his rag. "I'm asking you if the real reason you're canceling the show is that you think it won't do any good."

"Well, partly I'm canceling it because it isn't at all what I wanted it to be," said Maryellen. "I wrote a script, which no one appreciated at all! They just wanted to show off dancing and singing and lassoing Scooter. I had to give in and give in and give in, and now my part of the show is nothing."

"Ah, your pride is hurt," Dad said gently. "Was the purpose of the show to give you a chance to be a big famous star?"

"No!" said Maryellen. Then she said slowly, "Well, I did sort of want people to think of me as someone who

could make a difference in something important. So
I guess I wanted to be a little bit famous. Is that bad?"

"Not at all," said Dad.

"The purpose of the show was to raise money for
the March of Dimes and to encourage people to be vaccinated," said Maryellen.

"I see," said Dad. "That *is* a worthwhile purpose."
He turned away, picked up the hose, and gave Scooter a
hose-shower-bath, which Scooter loved.

Maryellen sighed. In all the disagreement and
excitement, she'd forgotten that what was truly important was the reason for the show: to fight polio.

"I think it's too late to uncancel the show now," she
said. "I pitched a big fit. Probably no one even wants to
do the show with me anymore."

"Maybe," said Dad. "You won't know unless you
ask."

Maryellen hesitated. Then she blurted out, "It will
be so humiliating. I'll have to call everyone, and apolo-
gize, and say that I'm canceling the cancellation, and
ask them to come tomorrow."

"Think you can do it?" asked Dad.

Maryellen shrugged and shook her head. "I dunno."

"Well, I think you can," said Dad, squirting the hose at her feet so that she had to smile.

"I'll give it a try," she said.

"That's my girl," said Dad. "You know what they say in show biz: The show must go on. Good luck."

"Thanks," said Maryellen. She took a deep breath. "Here goes nothing." She walked inside as if she had cement blocks on her feet instead of wet flip-flops, dreading apologizing to Carolyn and Beverly. What would she say?

But it turned out to be easy. As soon as Maryellen said that she was sorry, her sisters hugged her and said they were thrilled that the show was not cancelled. Carolyn celebrated by pounding out "Shake, Rattle and Roll" as loudly as she could on the piano, and Beverly danced wildly all around the living room. Tom and Mikey hadn't understood that the show was off in the first place, so they reacted calmly to the news that the show was on. They mostly just seemed glad that Maryellen was her usual nice, cheery self again.

Next Maryellen called Karen Stohlman, who let out a piercing shriek of joy and forgave her immediately and immediately insisted on calling Angela and Karen

King and telling them the good news. Luckily, no one had taken down any of the posters. So that left only one more thing to do, one more person she had to tell. *Actually*, she thought, squaring her shoulders, *two*.

It had been a long, long time since Maryellen had cut through the hedge between her house and the Fenstermachers'. She felt nervous. Through his bedroom window, she could see Davy gluing together pieces of a model airplane. It was reassuring to see that Davy still loved airplanes, as he had back when he and Maryellen were best friends.

Probably Davy wouldn't even remember their secret signal, Maryellen thought sadly. But she tapped on Davy's window anyway: *Tap, tappety, tap, tap. Tap, **tap***.

Davy flung his window open. "What's up, Doc?" he asked, just like the old days.

"Hey," said Maryellen. "Sorry I was such a pain before. We're going to do the show tomorrow, and I hope you still want to be in it. So, please come. I mean, only if you want to."

"Okay," said Davy without hesitating.

Maryellen felt flooded with relief and gratitude. "Good," she said. "Now, about Wayne. He's a pain, but everyone thinks that he's a funny pain. Do you think if I call him and say I'm sorry I hurt his feelings that he'll agree to be in the show?"

"Try and stop him," said Davy with a grin.

Maryellen grinned, too, in spite of herself. "Do you know his phone number?"

"Yup," said Davy. "It's 4628. You can remember it by saying four plus six is ten, take away two is eight."

"Or you could say, 'Four! Six! Two! Eight! Who do we appreciate?'" joked Maryellen. And she and Davy both said together, "Wayne!"

"Thank you, Davy," Maryellen said. "See you tomorrow."

"You bet," said Davy. "See you later, alligator."

"In a while, crocodile," Maryellen replied.

As she slipped back through the hedge to her own house, she realized that was the longest conversation she'd had with Davy since their fight back at the beginning of the school year. It was good to know that even if Davy wasn't her best friend anymore, he wasn't her enemy. He was on her side. Maryellen felt as though she had received one really nice birthday present already.

Maryellen made herself go straight to the telephone and dial 4-6-2-8.

Wayne answered. "Philpott's Pizza Parlor," he said. "Want-a-piece-a-pizza-pie?"

"Uh, no," said Maryellen, who knew that Wayne's family didn't really run a pizza parlor; his dad sold refrigerators. "Listen, Wayne, this is Ellie," she said, all in a rush. "I'm sorry about today. I hope you'll be in the show tomorrow. And, well, I hope you'll do your funny silent act behind me."

"Righto," Wayne said, putting on a fake British accent. "Jolly good. Pip, pip. Spot on."

"Okay, thanks," said Maryellen. "Bye."

"Cheerio," said Wayne.

And that was that. Maryellen wasn't exactly thrilled that Wayne was going to be in the show, but everyone else thought he was funny, and at least he didn't say anything during the performance, so he couldn't do too much harm. At least, she hoped not.

Who Do We Appreciate?

lthough Maryellen was exhausted when she went to bed, she just could not get to sleep. Too many ideas and worries and last-minute details and little things she must not forget to do were in her head, as prickly as pins and needles.

Pins and needles . . . Suddenly, Maryellen sat up. There was one great big important thing she had forgotten: her dress!

Mom had designated a corner of the living room as her sewing area so that she could watch TV and sew at the same time. Maryellen tiptoed out into the living room, which was dark and silent now, and turned on the little light on Mom's sewing machine. She wanted to see how close her dress was to being finished.

Gingerly, Maryellen picked up the material. It was recognizable as a dress, anyway. *Maybe I can finish it myself,* she thought. The dress needed to be hemmed, the sash needed to be attached, and the collar still looked backward. There was nothing she could do about the collar, but if she taped the hem up and safety-pinned the sash on, she could wear the dress in the show and as long as she didn't move around too much, it wouldn't fall apart and no one would know that it wasn't quite finished.

Maryellen went to the kitchen to get tape. When she got back to the living room, Joan was there. Joan had one finger stuck between the pages of her book, and she was peering down at Maryellen's dress, running her free hand over the skirt. She jumped when she saw Maryellen. "Yikes!" Joan whispered. "You startled me. What are you doing up? Wait, don't tell me. You're going to finish your bridesmaid dress—with tape?"

"Just the hem," said Maryellen quickly, "just temporarily, so I can wear it in the show tomorrow. Mom didn't have time to finish the hem or the sash, probably because she's been so busy with all the other wedding things."

"Oh," groaned Joan. "Mom's letting my wedding get out of hand. I keep telling her that Jerry and I don't want a big deal, but she won't listen, and she's knocking herself out over it. I wish I could tell her to *stop*."

"You want me to stop?" asked Mom, suddenly appearing from the hallway.

Joan dropped her book and rushed over to hug Mom. "Not everything, of course," she said. "But the things that are too hard and headachy for you to do, *yes*."

Mom smiled sadly. "I guess making the bridesmaid dresses is a headache," she said. "I had better turn that job over to a real seamstress." Mom tilted her head as she looked at the straps of Maryellen's dress. "Did I sew that collar on backward, or is it upside-down? Ah, well. I'm not very good at sewing, evidently."

"It's all right, Mom," Maryellen reassured her. "You're good at other things."

Joan and Mom laughed, and Mom said, "I guess I got carried away with the details and lost sight of the big picture."

"You know what? I sort of did the same thing about my show, Mom," said Maryellen. "Sometimes it's easy to forget the reason for something and get all twisted up in the details."

"Your show!" said Mom. "Oh dear. What will you

wear in your show tomorrow if you can't wear your bridesmaid dress, Ellie?"

"I'll think of something," said Maryellen, hiding her disappointment.

"I know!" said Joan. "How about my pink prom dress? It'll be a little big, but we can pin it, or . . ." She smiled at Maryellen, "tape it! It was my very first prom dress. Remember?"

"Of course I remember," said Maryellen. She had a fleeting flash of sorrow; though the pink dress was pretty, it wasn't hers. But she said gratefully, "Thanks, Joan. I'd love to wear it."

"Problem solved," said Mom, hanging Maryellen's unfinished bridesmaid dress on a hanger. "Now can we all please go to bed? Tomorrow is a big day. Birthday girls need their beauty sleep, especially one who's putting on a show."

Mom turned off the little sewing-machine light, and the living room was dark and silent once more. As Joan and Maryellen walked down the hallway to their room, Joan said softly, "You are going to look like a million bucks in that pink prom dress tomorrow, Ell-a-reenie. Wait and see."

✳

Maryellen peeked between the two sheets that were serving as curtains to hide backstage, which was really the carport. She looked out at the people who'd gathered on the driveway. Quite a good-sized crowd had come to see the show. Mrs. Stohlman, Mrs. King, and Mrs. Fenstermacher sat in beach chairs in the back row, laughing and talking a mile a minute with Angela's mother and grandmother. Wayne's parents, Mr. and Mrs. Philpott, had come, too. Mr. Philpott had a Kodak movie camera, and he was standing at the very end of the driveway, filming people as they dropped their dimes into the empty coffee can to pay their admission. There was a lanky teenage boy sitting next to Joan and Jerry whom Maryellen did not recognize at first. Then she realized it was Douglas Newswander, who'd danced with Carolyn at the sock hop. Families from the neighborhood had come, as well as eight girls from Maryellen's Girl Scout troop and six kids from her class at school. Scooter seemed to think that he was master of ceremonies and sashayed from person to person, graciously allowing everyone to pat him on the head while he drooled on their laps.

✳ Who Do We Appreciate? ✳

"Scooter!" Maryellen whispered from behind the curtain. "Come!"

But Scooter just made himself comfortable right in the middle of the stage and refused to budge. Maryellen had no choice but to step over Scooter when she went in front of the curtain to say "Welcome to our show." Then she had to step over him backward when she went behind the curtain again.

Naturally, however, Scooter wandered away when Angela and Karen King came out in their matching poodle skirts to sing "How Much Is That Doggie in the Window?" So Maryellen had to be the dog with the waggedy tail, swinging Davy's rope behind her, after all. It actually turned out to be a good thing that she was onstage, because Angela and Karen King had not learned all the words to the song, so Maryellen sang really loud when they came to a part they didn't know. The audience clapped and cheered, and Angela and Karen King curtsied and smiled while Maryellen darted backstage, gave Davy his rope, and then came back onstage so that Davy could lasso her. The audience oohed and ahhed every time Davy made the rope swoop over his head and then loop around her.

Tom and Mikey's puppet act was next. The little boys were supposed to crouch behind a box and move their puppets around while Maryellen told a story. But Mikey stood up and waved his hand with the puppet on it to the audience. Everyone laughed and clapped and cheered so much that Tom stood up and waved his puppet, too, so Maryellen gave up on telling any story, and let the little boys smile and wave until Carolyn began to play the music for Karen Stohlman and Beverly's ballet dance. The music was nice and loud, even though the piano was inside the house. Maryellen stood still as a statue while Karen and Beverly flitted around her and leaned on her for support, and then leapt off the stage, their tutus fluttering prettily.

The audience stamped their feet and clapped to the beat while Carolyn played "Shake, Rattle and Roll." At the end, Douglas Newswander shouted *Encore!* over and over until Carolyn played another song, "Heart and Soul." This time, the whole audience sang along. Carolyn knew that song by heart, so she didn't need Maryellen to turn pages of any sheet music, which was a good thing because it gave Maryellen time to run to her room to change.

Maryellen flew into her bedroom and then screeched to a halt. She couldn't believe her eyes when she saw what was hanging on her closet door. It wasn't the pink prom dress. It was her gorgeous green bridesmaid dress. Finished! Perfect! The hem was hemmed, the sash was attached, and the collar was front-side-front. Pinned to the dress was a note:

Dear Ellie,
     A darling girl in a darling show deserves her own darling dress.
Love,
Mrs. Fenstermacher

Maryellen's heart was filled with joy and gratitude as she slipped the dress over her head. *Mom must have asked Mrs. Fenstermacher to finish it this morning,* she realized, *while the rest of us were hurrying around getting ready for the show.* She allowed herself one quick glance at herself in the mirror—oh, the dress was lovely!—and then she had to race back to the stage. Everything was happening so fast! It was time for her speech about Jonas Salk, which meant that the show was nearly over.

When, lifting the hem of her skirt gracefully, she stepped out from between the curtains, the audience gasped in admiration at the sight of her in the snazzy green dress. Maryellen smiled a special smile at Mrs. Fenstermacher, who waved back.

Wheet-whoo! Dad whistled.

Maryellen blushed. Then she tried to begin her speech, but it came out all squeaky. "Fighting," she said in a tight, high voice. She tried again, "Fighting—" She swallowed hard. "Uh . . ."

"Polio!" Karen King whispered loudly, prompting from behind the curtains. "You're supposed to say, 'Fighting Polio.'"

Maryellen knew what she was supposed to say, but somehow she could not. As a matter of fact, she couldn't seem to say anything. Her mouth was dry. Her legs were as shaky as Jell-O. Her brain was empty. And her heart was thumping wildly. She wished Davy would lasso her and haul her off the stage. What on earth was the matter with her? She should have confidence; wasn't she wearing the most beautiful dress she'd ever worn? And she knew absolutely everyone in the audience, for Pete's sake. They were all friends and family. And yet when she looked at them all looking at her and waiting for her to speak, she couldn't move a muscle. The only sound was the ominous whirring of Mr. Philpott's movie camera. Unexpectedly, horribly, nightmarishly, Maryellen was frozen with stage fright.

She felt as though she'd been standing there for hours and hours, trembling in agony, unable to speak or move or even breathe, when suddenly Wayne thrust his head out between the curtains. Never in a million years would Maryellen have thought she'd be glad to see Wayne, but she definitely was right now. He looked so funny with his upside-down glasses and his hair sticking out all over his head that the audience chuckled. They laughed even more when he pretended to get his feet all tangled up in the curtains as he fought his way onto the stage.

"Hey!" Wayne said to Maryellen. "Do you know who I am?" She could only look at him, wide-eyed, as if she had never seen him before in her life. But it didn't matter, because Wayne chattered on, giving the information that Maryellen was supposed to give but could not. "I'm Dr. Jonas Salk, that's who. And do you know what I invented?"

Maryellen opened her mouth, but nothing came out.

"I invented a vaccine that prevents polio," said Wayne. He turned to the audience. "Now you all know that polio is a terrible, terrible disease. It hurts millions of people, especially children, and makes them very sick and sometimes, they can't ever walk again. Now, at last, after many years of research, I have found a safe vaccine to protect you from polio. So . . ." Wayne flung his arms out wide and sang,

> *Get a shot so you won't catch*
> *Poh-lee, oh-lee, oh!*

Then he said, "Come on, everybody! All together now!" All the cast members crowded out onto the stage. Wayne waved his arms as if he were conducting an orchestra and led them and the audience in singing,

> *Get a shot so you won't catch*
> *Poh-lee, oh-lee, oh!*

The audience stood up and cheered. Scooter howled. Wayne took exaggerated bows, and then rose up on his toes, waving his clasped hands over his head like a winning prizefighter, which made the audience laugh and clap even more.

Maryellen managed to smile at Wayne. It was a weak, watery smile, but it was humble and sincere.

Wayne cheerfully thumped her on the back, and then bowed to make the audience applaud him some more.

✳

After the show, Mom served birthday cake and lemonade. Dad surprised everyone by asking the Good Humor man to park his truck in the Larkins' driveway so that he could buy ice cream bars for them all.

Maryellen, who'd changed out of her dress, was sitting in the shade and eating her cake with Karen King, Angela, and Davy, when Karen Stohlman came over.

"Gosh," said Karen Stohlman, "what on earth happened to you, Ellie?" Karen's lips were circled in chocolate, and luckily, she too had changed and wasn't wearing her tutu, because her ice-cream-on-a-stick had dripped onto her shorts. "You were standing out there on the stage like a mummy."

Maryellen shuddered, remembering. "Stage fright, I guess," she said.

"Poor you!" said Angela. "I thought you were going to faint."

"Well, Wayne sure came to your rescue," said Karen Stohlman.

"Wayne saved the whole show," said Karen King.

"Yes," said Maryellen. "I never thought I'd say this, but thank goodness for Wayne!"

Davy grinned and chanted, "Four-six-two-eight! Who do we appreciate?"

And all five kids said, "Wayne!"

"Where is Wayne, by the way?" Maryellen asked.

Davy tilted his head toward the stage. There was Wayne. He had Beverly's tutu on his head and Karen Stohlman's tutu around his waist on top of his pants, and he was imitating the ballet they had danced in the show, while his father filmed him.

The Parade

hing, ching, ching. The dimes made a cheerful jingly sound as Maryellen poured them out of the coffee can onto the kitchen table. Everyone had gone home, and all the Larkins were sitting in the kitchen Saturday evening while Maryellen counted the money the show had earned.

"So many people came today!" said Beverly as Maryellen added up the dimes.

"I bet we earned twenty-eleven dollars!" said Tom.

Maryellen grinned. "Not quite that much," she said. "We earned three dollars and twenty cents."

"Bravo!" cheered Dad and Joan.

"That's a respectable amount," said Carolyn. "You should be happy, Ellie."

"I agree," said Mom. "I'll give you three dollar bills for thirty dimes, dear. And I'll even contribute an envelope and the money you'll need for a stamp. You had better take your envelope to the post office and have it weighed. It might cost extra because of the two dimes in it."

"That'll be great, Mom," said Maryellen. "Three dollars and twenty cents isn't a fortune, but it's something, and—" She grinned at Dad, "something is always better than nothing."

"Hear, hear," said Dad.

Maryellen felt very efficient and grown-up as she paper-clipped the three dollar bills to a piece of paper and taped the two dimes underneath them. She wrote:

Dear March of Dimes,

All my friends and I are so glad Dr. Salk found a polio vaccine! Here is some money to buy shots for people, especially children.

Sincerely yours,

Maryellen Larkin

She addressed the envelope to the local March of Dimes headquarters in Daytona Beach, and it was ready to go. Since the next day was Sunday, when the post office would be closed, she would mail the money on Monday.

✳

On Monday, Maryellen hurried home from school. Mom was making a snack for Tom and Mikey, so she had one, too. Beverly and Carolyn had just joined them when the phone rang.

"Ellie, it's for you," said Carolyn, holding out the receiver. "It's some man."

Maryellen took the phone. "Hello?"

"Maryellen, this is Dr. Oser," the man said. "Today, five children came to my office to be vaccinated with the polio vaccine. Their mothers said that the children had seen your show and that's why they came to get their shots. So I'm calling to thank you!"

"You're welcome," stammered Maryellen, a little shyly.

"One child brought a poster with him," Dr. Oser went on. "It was one of the posters that you made to advertise your show. I was wondering if you'd make another poster about getting vaccinated, so I could hang it up in my office."

"Me? You want a poster by *me*?" Maryellen squeaked.

"Yes, indeed," said Dr. Oser. "Bring it to my office in the Medical Building on Drayton Street whenever it's ready. I'd like to meet you."

"Well, okay, sure!" said Maryellen.

"Good," said Dr. Oser. "And thank you, Maryellen. You've done something important by encouraging these kids to get their shots. Good-bye."

"Bye," said Maryellen.

"Who was that?" asked Mom.

"It was a doctor who said that five kids got shots today because of our show," crowed Maryellen, bouncing on her toes. "And he wants me to make another polio poster for his office."

"Holy cow!" exclaimed Carolyn.

"Ellie!" breathed Beverly. "You're *famous*."

Mom hugged Maryellen. "That's wonderful, sweetie," she said. "Dad and I are so proud of you! Off you go now, to the post office to mail your money."

"I'll come with you," said Carolyn.

"I want to go, too!" said Beverly.

Naturally, Tom and Mikey wanted to come, and that meant Scooter, too, so there was quite a crowd gathered behind Maryellen as she handed her envelope to the lady at the post office.

"Please, may I buy a stamp for this?" Maryellen asked politely.

"Sure, honey," said the lady behind the counter. She looked at the address. "March of Dimes, eh?"

"It's money!" Beverly piped up. "And we earned it ourselves. We put on a show with the Karens and Angela and Davy and Wayne. I danced, and Carolyn played rock 'n' roll—"

"And we did puppets!" interrupted Tom, pointing to Mikey and himself.

"You don't say," said the lady, smiling.

"It was all Ellie's idea," Beverly rattled on, scattering facts in no particular order. "She wrote a show but no one liked it, so then she helped everyone in all the other acts. It was her birthday party. She's ten now. And today a doctor called and said kids got polio shots because of her show, and he wants her to make a poster for his office."

"My word!" said the lady. "That's a very impressive contribution to our community. Not every ten-year-old kid in the world would do that for her birthday. You should be proud of yourself, Miss—" she looked at the envelope in her hand—"Maryellen Larkin."

"Thank you," said Maryellen, pink in the face.

"No, thank you, Maryellen," said the lady. "It'll be an honor to mail this letter for you."

✶

A few days later, the phone rang. "I'll get it," Carolyn hollered. She always ran to answer the phone these days. Most of the time it was Douglas Newswander calling her. But apparently this time it wasn't. "Ellie," Carolyn called out. "Phone for you."

Maryellen thought it was probably Dr. Oser, so she was surprised when a high, fluty voice said, "Hello. Is this Miss Maryellen Larkin?"

"Uh, yes . . ." Maryellen hesitated. Then she snorted, "Har-dee har, har, Wayne. Very funny." She was sure that it was Wayne, making a prank phone call in one of his silly voices. But why was Wayne calling her?

"Excuse me," said the voice, sounding even higher and flutier. "This is Betty Plotnick, the secretary for the mayor of Daytona Beach. Am I speaking to Miss Maryellen Larkin?"

"Cut it out, Wayne," said Maryellen. "Stop goofing

around. I know it's you."

"No, this is Bet-ty Plot-nick," said the voice, pro-
nouncing the words slowly, as if speaking to someone
who wasn't quite right in the head. "I need to speak to
Ma-ry-ell-en Lar-kin, please."

Suddenly it dawned on Maryellen that maybe it
wasn't Wayne after all. "Oh, I'm sorry!" she sputtered,
wishing that she could sink into a pit. "This is Maryellen."

"Good!" said the woman. "The mayor of Daytona
Beach would like to invite you to ride in the Memorial
Day parade with him in his convertible."

"Do what?" gasped Maryellen. "I mean, thank you,
I'd love to! But why?"

"In recognition of your support for the March of
Dimes," said Betty Plotnick. "The mayor's office has had
three letters about you: one from a Dr. Ron Oser, one
from Miss Evelyn Danziger of the U.S. Post Office, and
one from a Mr. David Fenstermacher, who wrote to the
March of Dimes, and they forwarded his letter on to us."

"Davy wrote a letter?" asked Maryellen.

Betty Plotnick went on, "The mayor is impressed
with your sense of responsibility and the fine example
you set for the young people of our town. Please come

to City Hall at eight a.m. on Memorial Day. Good-bye!"

✳

Boom, thumped the drums. *Toot-tootle-toot-toot*, blasted the trumpets. *Whoosh, snap, flap*, fluttered the flags in the warm Memorial Day morning breeze.

"Hurray!" cheered the crowds lining the streets as Maryellen waved to them from the mayor's convertible.

It was easy not to have stage fright in the parade, because she didn't have to say anything. Even when the newspaper reporter had interviewed her before the parade, all she'd had to say was her name. The mayor told all the rest of the story about her show. Then the newspaper reporter took a photo of Maryellen and the mayor sitting in the convertible. On the sides of the convertible were signs that said:

Maryellen Larkin
Youngest March of Dimes Fund-Raiser
in Daytona Beach!

As the parade moved on, Maryellen could see the silvery flash of batons and the gold flash of cymbals up ahead as the high school marching band led the way. Colorful balloons bobbed in the air, and people tossed confetti and rose petals that landed softly on her shoulders and in her lap. There was a bagpipe band of men wearing kilts, a precision drill team of ladies on horseback, a fleet of fire engines, floats decorated with crepe-paper flowers, a man dressed as Uncle Sam on stilts, and clowns riding tiny tricycles. It was a terrific parade!

Maryellen smiled and waved as she passed the reviewing stand, which was decked out in red-white-and-blue bunting. Seated in the reviewing stand were dignitaries and veterans from World Wars One and Two and the Korean War.

Maryellen's smile grew even wider, her wave was even more enthusiastic, and her heart filled with happiness when she saw her own family lined up along the street. Mikey was on Dad's shoulders, Mom held Tom up so that he could see, and Joan, Jerry, Carolyn, Douglas, and Beverly stood all in a row. Even Scooter was sitting at attention on the curb, looking unusually alert and perky, for Scooter. The Karens and Angela were there, too, and Davy and Wayne, all wildly waving little American flags.

"Hurray, Ellie!" they shouted. "Hurray, hurray, hurray!"

Maryellen twisted around so that she could wave to them even after her car had passed them by. She could hear them cheering still, long after her car had turned the corner and they couldn't see her anymore. Maryellen sat up straight, and waved to the crowd, and thought there could be no happier ten-year-old than she was in the whole wide world.

A Star

bsolutely great.

That's how it felt to be famous. Maryellen had always wondered, and now she knew. Ever since she'd had her picture in the newspaper in the Memorial Day parade riding in a convertible with the mayor of Daytona Beach, everyone knew who she was.

"Gosh, Ellie," gushed Karen King. "You're a star."

"You're the most famous girl in Daytona Beach," Angela added.

"And we are your friends," said Karen Stohlman proudly.

Maryellen blushed and smiled, shrugging off her friends' compliments. But she knew that the compliments were true. Take right now, for instance. Maryellen, the two Karens, and Angela were on the playground before school playing hopscotch, and a little cluster of

Maryellen's fans stood watching. They clapped when she threw her marker well or completed her turn without stepping on any chalk lines. The applause made her feel like a movie star even though she was sort of getting used to it. Whenever she walked down the hall at school, kids she didn't even know—big sixth-graders, even— waved and said, "Hi, Ellie." Shyer kids just smiled. Little kids stared, nudged one another as she passed by, and whispered, "That's Maryellen Larkin, the one who was in the parade. Her picture was in the newspaper."

It felt great to be famous; she knew that she'd feel let down when it ended. And it would end soon, because today was the last day of school.

Although Maryellen loved school, the idea of the summer stretching out ahead was thrilling. Summer— full of books and swimming and hide-and-seek after dark and picnics and running through the sprinkler and watching fireflies and eating Popsicles—was the best. At least, it used to be. This year felt different.

"You know," she said, "the last day of school is right up there with my birthday and Christmas as one of my favorite days of the year. But today, I'm sort of sorry that it's the last day of school."

✳ A Star ✳

"You're going to miss all the attention, that's why," said Karen King.

Maryellen nodded. As usual, Karen King was right. Oh, it was satisfying to be admired and envied! Maryellen walked around feeling as though her feet were six inches off the ground, even when she was not playing hopscotch!

Just then the bell rang and it was time to go inside. Maryellen put her marker in her pocket and gently picked up her gift for Mrs. Humphrey. Every year, Maryellen made a present to give to her teacher on the last day of school. This year, she had made cookies in the shape of starfish and a card with a picture of the ocean on it. She had written on the card:

For Mrs. Humphrey,
   You are a great teacher.
Love,
Maryellen Larkin

Maryellen's cursive handwriting was still a little slapdash. The *r* was a little too close to the *m*, so it looked as if the card said "*ForM rs. Humphrey.*" Also, some of the legs of some of the starfish cookies had broken off, but Mom had said that happened to real starfish, too, and the cookies would still taste fine, so Maryellen felt pretty happy as she put the paper plate carefully on Mrs. Humphrey's desk with the other gifts. Karen Stohlman's gift was a superior-looking store-bought present in a rectangular box that was gift-wrapped and tied with curly ribbons. Wayne put his gift, which was a seashell, on top of it. The seashell was still rather wet and sandy and beginning to smell. So Maryellen felt that her gift fell right in the middle, in terms of how good it was.

"Thank you for your gifts, boys and girls," said Mrs. Humphrey, over and over again. "Please be seated." But it was like trying to calm a herd of wild horses because the students were so excited that it was the last day. They could just barely contain their exuberance. Wayne stood on his chair and chanted:

> *No more pencils,*
> *No more books,*
> *No more teachers'*
> *Dirty looks!*

✴ A Star ✴

"Ah, Wayne!" sighed Mrs. Humphrey. "How I will miss you!"

Everybody laughed. They knew that Mrs. Humphrey meant the exact opposite of what she'd said.

Mrs. Humphrey was clearly glad to turn the class over to Mr. Carey, the principal, and Mr. Hagopian, one of the fifth-grade teachers, when they entered the room just after the Pledge of Allegiance.

Everyone was wary of Mr. Carey, since he was the one who called parents when a kid got into trouble. They quieted down and even Wayne stopped wiggling when Mr. Carey said, "Boys and girls, give your attention to Mr. Hagopian."

Mr. Hagopian stepped forward. The top of his bald head was cheerfully pink and shiny, and so were his cheeks and his nose. "Because you are going to be in the fifth grade next year, you are eligible to be in the Science Club," he announced. "I hope you will join, because the Daytona Beach school district is sponsoring a science contest. Students can team up today and then meet about their projects over the summer. In the fall, the projects will be judged and the winners will be chosen. Our school is hosting the contest, so we want to have an impressive turnout."

"You kids have got to keep your brains awake over the summer!" Mr. Carey chimed in. "You can't let those Communist kids in Russia get ahead of you!"

Maryellen and her classmates weren't terribly impressed by this; they were used to being told that they were in competition against the Communists. But they were impressed when Mr. Hagopian said, "Students in the contest will invent a flying machine."

"Oooh," all the students murmured, as an electric current of excitement ran through the class. Recently, a rocket had been launched into outer space from Cape Canaveral, which was not far from Daytona Beach, so just about everybody was fascinated by the notion of rockets.

Wayne stood up and ruffled his hair and put his glasses on upside down, pretending to be a mad-scientist-inventor, just as he had in Maryellen's polio show. "I vill vin!" he said in a fake accent. Everyone laughed until Mr. Carey, who was well acquainted with Wayne, gave him a withering frown. Wayne meekly slid back down into his seat.

Mr. Hagopian went on, "All interested students are

invited to meet in my classroom after lunch today."

Maryellen bounced in her seat. She wished it were after lunch *already*, she felt so fired up about the contest!

With a gentle swoosh, a paper airplane landed on her desk. Maryellen knew it was from Davy. She turned around and grinned at him. Davy had always been interested in airplanes and things that fly and Maryellen always loved a challenge to her imagination, so, without saying a word, they knew that they'd both join in the contest.

But at lunch, Maryellen's other friends had lots of words to say—mostly discouraging ones—when she announced, "I am so excited about the science contest!"

"Why on earth would you want to do an extra science project, of all things?" asked Karen King. "I mean, that's like giving yourself homework over the summer!"

"I would take part in the contest," said Karen Stohlman. The other three girls slid sideways glances at one another. They knew that Karen Stohlman liked to copycat Maryellen. "But what with Girl Scout camp, swimming lessons, and ballet," she went on, "I'm going to be too busy."

"I think the contest sounds like fun," Angela said, "but I'm going to Italy to visit my relatives, so I won't be able to meet with a team over the summer. Maybe I'll join the club in the fall, though."

"Not me!" said Karen King. "Watch out, Ellie," she cautioned. "You're not going to know anybody in the club. Probably the only kids who will show up at the meeting today will be older boys."

"I bet that's right," agreed Karen Stohlman. "And they'll be drips who read science-fiction comic books."

Maryellen's enthusiasm wavered for a moment. She understood that the Karens were warning her that if she joined the Science Club, she would be regarded as strange. Most kids thought it was weird for girls to like science.

Just then, Davy tapped her on the shoulder. "Come on!" he said. He looked so excited that Maryellen's doubts disappeared.

"See you later!" she said to the Karens and Angela. As she jumped up from the lunch table to follow Davy, her enthusiasm was only slightly dimmed by the fact that Wayne, wearing his helicopter beanie hat, was glued to Davy's side as always.

✳ A Star ✳

Maryellen was a little embarrassed to walk into Mr. Hagopian's fifth-grade classroom with Wayne spinning the propeller on his beanie, because she immediately saw that the Karens were right: Most of the kids were boys who were going to be in the sixth grade next fall. There were only two other girls there. One girl Maryellen didn't know at all, and the other girl she vaguely recognized as someone who took piano lessons at the same place as Carolyn.

As Maryellen took a seat, she heard the now-familiar murmur of recognition, "That's Maryellen Larkin!" She sat up straight, feeling self-conscious but a little better.

"Settle down, kids," said Mr. Hagopian. "Today, I'll divide you into teams. Your task at this first meeting is to brainstorm. Over the summer, you'll flesh out your ideas. Your team will choose the best one and build your flying machine in the early fall, and then you'll be ready for the contest. Any questions?"

A big boy called out, "Is it true that the contest winners will be interviewed on television?"

Mr. Hagopian's bald spot got a little pinker and shinier as he said, "Yes!"

Well, thought Maryellen, *that settles it!* Now she

was more excited than ever. For as long as she could remember, she had imagined herself on television. And she couldn't help thinking that if she appeared on television as a science star, her fame would *never* fade.

Mr. Hagopian divided the kids into teams by the simple method of splitting the classroom in half. Maryellen found herself the only girl on a team with Davy, Wayne, and four older boys.

A big boy named Skip immediately took control. "Okay, guys," he said, looking only at the older boys as if Maryellen, Davy, and Wayne were invisible. "I was in the Rocket Club. So let's just save time and say I'm captain of our team. We'll call ourselves the Sixth-Grade Launchmen."

"Just a second," Maryellen protested meekly. "Don't we get to vote or anything?" She looked around, but only Davy seemed to share her indignation at how bossy Skip was.

Skip glanced at Maryellen. "You take notes." He handed her a piece of paper. "Write on the back of this."

"Notes? But why—" Maryellen stammered, taken aback. It was bad enough that Skip had dismissed her—and Davy, too—lumping them together with helicopter-head Wayne as lowly still-really-fourth-graders. But by casting her in the supporting role of secretary, Skip made it seem as if she were not an equal member of the team but someone who was there only to record other people's ideas. "How come I have to take notes?"

"You're the girl," said Skip, as if the connection between being a girl and being a secretary was obvious.

"Well, I know, but that doesn't mean—" Maryellen began, but the Sixth-Grade Launchmen had already launched themselves into a loud conversation about their flying-machine ideas.

As the boys talked right over her, Maryellen sighed and looked at the paper that Skip had given her. At the top it said "Rules of the Contest." That sounded important. She began to read and as she did, she saw one rule in particular that she thought the rest of her team needed to know about. "Hey, guys!" she said. "You should—" But no one listened to her, so she gave up.

Maryellen loved to doodle, so as she listened to the boys pitch their ideas, she made sketches on the blank side of the rules sheet of what they were describing. She was quicker and better at sketching than at writing—her handwriting was never very good—and besides, she was not going to take notes, no matter what bossy Skip said. To listen to the boys argue about whose idea was best, you'd think the contest part of the contest had started already!

"Let's make bird wings!" said one boy. "I'll strap 'em on and fly."

"No, let's make our flying machine in the shape of a football, and I'll toss it," said another boy, demonstrating his throwing arm.

"Let's build a kite, and then cut off the string when it's flying high," said Davy.

"That's baby stuff!" scoffed another boy. "Let's build a B-52 bomber!"

"Or a helicopter!" Wayne contributed, flicking the propeller on his beanie to make it spin and pretending to be lifted up.

"Wait, what?" said Maryellen, dismayed at how bad the ideas were. Davy's kite idea was the only idea that sounded the least bit practical. The rest of the ideas all sounded impossible. But the boys weren't listening to one another, so they certainly wouldn't listen to her.

Maryellen was relieved when Mr. Hagopian called

out, "Okay, kids! Time's up. Go back to your classrooms. Let's meet at the same time next week at the
public library. See you then. Keep it down to a dull roar
in the hallway, please."

Quietly, Maryellen folded the paper with the rules
on one side and her sketches on the other. She put it in
her pocket as she and Wayne and Davy headed back
down the long, cool, dim hallway to Mrs. Humphrey's
room.

It was a last-day-of-school tradition for the students
to have Popsicles while they emptied out their desks
and their cubbies in the cloakroom. Soon, everybody's
lips were purple, orange, or red, depending on the
flavor of Popsicle they'd had. It was another tradition
for the teachers to go outside first and line up on either
side of the doors. As the students burst out of the building, the teachers clapped and cheered for them and
patted them on the back. The buses honked their horns,
and the kids climbed on, waving out the windows and
yelling, "Good-bye!" As the buses pulled out, walk-
ers like Maryellen ran along the sidewalk waving and
cheering until the buses turned the corner.

Davy walked his bike next to Maryellen on the way

home. Mr. Carey was having a little "let's do better next year" conference with Wayne, so it was just Maryellen and Davy for a change.

"How come you were so quiet in the meeting?" Davy asked.

Maryellen shrugged. "Just gave up trying to be heard, I guess."

"You? Give up?" said Davy. "Nuh-uh."

Maryellen laughed. "I did have a few ideas, but it seemed like if I suggested them, the big boys would, you know, shoot 'em down."

"You were afraid they'd go over like *lead balloons*," joked Davy. "Skip would say they weren't *topflight*!"

Maryellen chimed in. "They'd never *get off the ground*."

"I don't think any of the ideas the boys talked about today will get off the ground," said Davy, getting serious. "We've got to come up with better ideas—something that'll really take off—if we're going to win the contest."

"Taking off is only part of the problem," said Maryellen. "The winner has to stay in the air the longest." She pulled the sheet of contest rules out of her pocket and handed it to Davy. "Read this."

Davy read. "Uh-oh," he said.

"You can say that again," said Maryellen. She grinned at Davy. "I think you and I had better talk more at the next meeting. We'd better tell the boys the rules, or else the Launchmen will be the Loser-men for sure."

Flabbergasted

CHAPTER SEVEN

Yahoo!" shrieked Maryellen.

To celebrate the last day of school, Mom had cut up a chilled watermelon and set up the oscillating sprinkler in the front yard. Within minutes of being home from school, Maryellen and Beverly were in their bathing suits running through the deliciously cold sprinkler water. Tom and Mikey danced from foot to foot just at the edge of the spray, and whenever the cold water rained down on them gently, they closed their eyes and squealed with delight. Scooter, lying with his head on his paws, watched from the shade.

The kids were having a contest to see who could spit their watermelon seeds the farthest when suddenly Beverly said, with wide eyes, "Look!"

Maryellen's mouth fell open in flabbergasternation. Dad was turning in to their driveway, and attached to his car was a huge silver trailer. Dad honked the car horn, and Mom, Joan, and Carolyn came dashing out of the house. Mom had a dust rag in her hand, Joan had a book, and Carolyn had a hairbrush. Half of her hair was up in pin curls and the other half hung down wet.

"Dad, Dad, Dad, Dad, Dad!" hollered Tom. As Dad got out of the car, Tom hurled himself into his arms and Dad swung him around exuberantly. Scooter howled to add to the commotion, and Mikey clung to Scooter and howled, too.

"What on earth is *that*?" asked Mom, flapping her dust rag at the trailer, when everyone had settled down a bit.

"Isn't it a beauty?" said Dad, patting the trailer proudly. "It's the 1955 Airstream. And it's all ours. We are going to see the U.S.A. this summer, kids, and this will be our home away from home."

"Hurray!" cheered everyone but Mom.

"Can we go inside it?" Maryellen asked.

"Sure!" said Dad. He lifted Mikey and led the way, and everyone including Scooter followed him into the trailer.

"Ooooh," breathed all the kids. Inside, the Airstream

was shipshape and trim. The front end of the trailer to the right of the door was the living room; Maryellen had never seen anything so fabulously modern but also comfortable and homey. Tom was already bouncing on one of two plaid couches, and Mikey was hoisting Scooter up onto an easy chair. The kitchen was in the middle, just across from the door. It had a tiny sink, refrigerator, stove, and shelves.

"Look how darling the kitchen is!" cooed Carolyn. "It has everything a regular kitchen has, only miniature."

"Get a load of this, honey," Dad said to Mom. He opened a cupboard and pulled down an ironing board.

"I'm thrilled," said Mom, though she didn't sound as if she really was.

To the left of the kitchen were a bed and a closet, and the whole back end was a bathroom, which Joan was inspecting closely. Maryellen poked her head in, too. "There's even a bathtub and shower!" she exclaimed.

By this time, several neighbors had gathered in the Larkins' driveway to admire the Airstream. Maryellen was pleased that her family was the center of attention.

"What model did you buy, Stan?" asked Mr. Fenstermacher.

"The twenty-four-foot Trade Wind Double," said Dad.

"Top of the line," said Mr. Fenstermacher. "You could use it as a bomb shelter, for cryin' out loud. It has everything you'd need!"

"It looks like it could take off and fly," said Davy.

"It should," bragged Dad. He was an architect, so he appreciated good design that used space economically. "It was inspired by Charles Lindbergh's *Spirit of Saint Louis*, the first plane to fly nonstop across the Atlantic Ocean."

"Well, Ellie," said Davy. "If you go away, you'll miss the team meetings, but just being in the Airstream will give you good ideas about flying machines."

"You're right!" agreed Maryellen happily.

Finally, the excitement quieted down, the neighbors left, and Mom called the family to dinner. Everyone went inside reluctantly. Scooter refused to budge, and Maryellen didn't blame him. The house seemed awfully sprawling and dull compared with the sleek and snazzy Airstream.

Mom plunked a tuna-noodle casserole onto the table and then sat down and sighed.

"What's the matter, dear?" Dad asked.

"Well," said Mom, "I just wish that you had consulted me before you bought such a—well, such a whopping huge purchase. The Airstream is a Very Expensive Thing."

"I wanted it to be a surprise," said Dad.

"It's a surprise, all right," said Mom. "I never expected to have a gigantic silver rocket ship parked in our driveway."

"Oh, it won't be parked in our driveway for long," said Dad. "This summer, we're taking a family road trip. All the magazines say that family togetherness is very important."

Joan asked quickly, "How long will we be gone?"

"At least three weeks," said Dad.

"Three weeks?" repeated Joan. "Oh, Dad, I don't want to be away from Jerry for that long. And Mom was going to teach me how to cook. I'm getting married at the end of the summer, remember?"

"Of course I do, sweetheart," said Dad. "In fact, that's why I bought the Airstream: so that we could have one last road trip together as a family." Dad reached over and tousled Joan's hair fondly.

"A road trip?" asked Mom. "You mean we won't be

going to visit my parents?" Every summer before this, the Larkins had gone to the Georgia mountains to stay with Grandmom and Grandpop for vacation.

"Well," said Dad, "I thought we'd head out west, to Yellowstone National Park. It's high time the kids saw some of the wide-open spaces of the U.S.A. west of the Mississippi. All the magazines say that it's our patriotic duty as Americans to see as much as we can of this great country."

"I love the idea of heading west!" Maryellen gushed. Just about all of her favorite TV shows were Westerns. She pictured herself riding a galloping horse across the sagebrush prairie, sleeping out under the stars, and crossing raging rivers like the pioneers. "Please can we go to the Alamo, Dad?" she begged. "Davy Crockett was there." Maryellen and the little kids sang the song from the TV show:

> *Davy, Davy Crockett!*
> *King of the wild frontier!*

"Don't expect the West to still look the way it does in those ridiculous Westerns that you watch on TV," cautioned Joan. "And Davy Crockett? I can't believe you idolize a guy who walked around with a dead raccoon on his head."

Mom held up both hands to stop the whole discussion. She looked harried. "I've got Joan and Jerry's wedding breathing down my neck," she said to Dad. "There's still so much to do. The painters are coming next week to get the house ready for the wedding. Who'll supervise them—Scooter?"

"Scooter will come with us," said Dad. "And don't you think you'd like a vacation from all the wedding worries?"

"I'm not sure that it *will* be a vacation for me," said Mom. "Staying in a trailer in a campground just means that I'll be doing all my usual work of cooking and laundering and housekeeping and cleaning and even ironing under tougher-than-usual conditions."

Everyone was quiet, thinking about what Mom had said. Maryellen could see that Mom had several valid points. But she could also see that Dad was as excited about the trip as she and all the other kids were, except Joan.

"Mom," said Maryellen, "what if Grandmom and

Grandpop came *here*? That way, we could see them, and they could take care of the house while we're gone and be sure the painters are doing everything right. They could stay for a while after our trip, too, so that we could have a nice long visit together."

Mom considered her suggestion. "That might work," she said, nodding and smiling a little.

"That's a great idea, Ellie," said Dad, beaming.

Joan perked up. "I could stay here with Grandmom and Grandpop," she said.

"No!" Maryellen protested firmly. "You heard what Dad said about this being our last family trip. You have to come, Joan! You'll ruin it if you don't. Gosh, even Scooter is coming." Maryellen turned eagerly to Mom. "And I'll take care of Scooter on the trip, I promise." Truthfully, she didn't think that being responsible for lazy, sleepy Scooter would be very hard. Scooter was always easygoing and agreeable about everything except moving quickly. She added, "And I'll help with other chores, too."

"Me, too," promised Beverly and Tom in unison.

"Me!" said Mikey, who had no idea what was going on.

"I'll help, too," said Carolyn. "It'll be *fun* to keep the Airstream neat and tidy and shipshape!"

"You needn't worry about cooking much, sweet-heart," said Dad to Mom. "We'll mostly be eating the fish I catch. I'll fry 'em up over a campfire."

"We'll have s'mores for dessert," added Maryellen. "And you can teach Joan to cook in the little Airstream kitchen, and then *she* can make dinner for us, too."

"All right," said Mom. She shrugged in surrender. "Westward ho, I guess."

"Atta girl!" said Dad, hugging Mom. Everyone cheered, except Joan.

✶

The next few days were a hurricane of shopping, packing, gathering, and preparing. The whole family went to O'Neal's department store to buy long pants and warm jackets, because Dad said the weather would be cold at Yellowstone. Dad bought a tent and sleeping bags at the Army Navy store because there were not enough beds for everyone in the Airstream. Mom went to the grocery store to buy food for the trip. "In case the fish aren't biting," she said, winking at Dad.

✳ Flabbergasted ✳

Jerry, Joan's fiancé, drove the girls in his hot rod to the library to stock up on books. On the way home, he stopped at a diner and generously treated everyone to French fries and ketchup. Joan had to eat her French fries with one hand, because Jerry was holding her other hand, the one with the engagement ring on it. He had already put a nickel in the jukebox so that it would play their special song, "Sincerely," by the McGuire Sisters.

"I'm going to miss you, *sincerely*," said Jerry to Joan. "I wish you didn't have to go."

Beverly giggled, "Mushy." Maryellen kicked her leg under the table to shush her. She wanted to hear what Joan was going to say.

"I don't want to go," sighed Joan. "But Dad has his heart set on this being a whole-family trip. I can't let him down."

"You'll have lots of time to read, anyway," said Jerry. "I know how you love books." He smiled and squeezed Joan's hand. "I am a lucky guy, marrying a girl with brains *and* beauty."

Joan put her French fry hand on top of Jerry's and said, "I'll be thinking of you and missing you every mile of the way."

✳ Taking Off ✳

The look Jerry gave Joan was so sweetly romantic that Maryellen and Carolyn practically swooned.

✳

Everyone was excited and elated when Grandmom and Grandpop arrived. Grandpop insisted on sleeping in the Airstream, just to see what it was like. The next morning he said, "By gum, that trailer's a jim-dandy! Never slept better in my life. Your trip is going to be terrific." He patted Maryellen on the shoulder. "You're my correspondent, Ellie-girl. So don't forget to send me postcards." He sounded envious.

Maryellen, who knew that Grandpop loved maps and traveling as much as she did, promised to send him postcards of every place they visited.

The night before they left, Dad assigned each person one drawer in the Airstream. Mom was helping Maryellen fold her pajamas, underwear, shirts, pants, and shorts neatly and put them in her drawer—which was under the couch in the compact living room—when Grandmom knocked on the door of the trailer.

"Hello, dear heart," she said to Maryellen. "I have a present for you." She handed Maryellen a sketchbook.

"I remembered that when you visited Grandpop and me at Christmastime, you were interested in the birds that came to my bird feeder. So I thought you might like to draw sketches of some of the birds—and other things—that you see on your trip."

"Oh, thank you, Grandmom!" said Maryellen. She held the sketchbook out to her mother, saying, "Mom, look at the sketchbook that Grandmom gave me. I can fill it with drawings. Won't that be great?"

"It certainly will," said Mom.

"You know what?" Maryellen went on. "I'll draw my ideas for flying machines in this sketchbook, too."

"Flying machines?" asked Grandmom.

Maryellen nodded. "I'm in a school contest to invent the best flying machine," she explained.

"You don't say," said Grandmom. "You should consult with your mother. Remember, she worked in an aircraft factory during the war."

"Oh, right," said Maryellen, turning to Mom. "Do you have any good ideas for flying machines, Mom?"

"Well," said Mom. "I wasn't on the design team. But I remember that the designers were on the lookout for ideas all the time."

"I'll keep a pencil handy, and draw everything that flies," said Maryellen.

"Smart girl," said Mom, smiling. "The world is full of inspiration. But you have to be paying attention, looking and listening, all the time."

"The Launchmen team is not good at listening," sighed Maryellen.

"That's too bad," said Mom. "When I was a line manager at the aircraft factory, it was my job to be sure that everybody cooperated and worked together happily and well. That's how good work is done."

"Your mother did a wonderful job as manager," said Grandmom proudly. "She was so good, she was asked to stay on after the war."

"Why didn't you, Mom?" asked Maryellen.

"The factory directors and I had a difference of opinion," said Mom. "I thought that the women workers who wanted to keep their jobs should be able to, but the bosses felt the jobs should be given to men coming back from the war. It still makes me mad, because many of the women were supporting their families. I said I wouldn't stay if the other women were let go. So when they were fired, I left, too."

"Were you sorry?" asked Maryellen.

"I was sorry that the bosses were so stubborn and narrow-minded!" said Mom. "But I wasn't going to go along with something I didn't think was right. And I certainly didn't want to work for people who wouldn't listen to me or respect my ideas."

"Davy and I wish the Launchmen team would listen to *our* ideas," said Maryellen. "We really want to win the science contest. If we do, we'll be on TV!" Maryellen smiled at Grandmom. "Wouldn't you be proud of me?"

Grandmom's bright, dark eyes sparkled. "I'm already proud of you," she said. "Your mother told me about the show that you put on to raise money to fight polio."

"Wasn't that a fine thing for a young girl to do on her birthday?" said Mom.

"I was in the Memorial Day parade with the mayor," said Maryellen to Grandmom, "and my picture was in the newspaper, so now all the kids at school know who I am." She sighed. "It's great to be famous."

"Mmm," agreed Grandmom. "But isn't it what you're famous for that matters?"

"What do you mean?" asked Maryellen.

"Well, people are famous for all sorts of different things, which is just as it should be. But wouldn't you rather be famous for doing something that makes the world better—like fighting polio—than for being a bank robber, for instance?" said Grandmom. "That writer Joan is reading, Thoreau, said, 'Be not simply good; be good for something.' That way, even after your fame fades away and people forget who you are, what you *did* will still be there. In fact, you might even do something wonderful just because it's the right thing to do, even if it won't make you famous at all."

"So I shouldn't want to be on TV?" asked Maryellen, puzzled.

Grandmom kissed her on the forehead. "Whether or not you're ever on TV, you'll always be famous to me," she said.

"To me, too," said Mom. "Now you and Scooter had better trot along to bed so that you'll be ready to be 'good for something.'" She hugged Maryellen and joked, "If you don't get enough sleep, you'll be good-for-nothings."

Songs of the Open Road

his land is your land, this land is my land,
From California to the New York Island,
From the redwood forest
To the Gulf Stream waters,
This land was made for you and me!

Maryellen sang at the top of her voice, and so did Carolyn and Beverly, and even Mom and Dad. Tom and Mikey didn't know the words, so whenever they felt like it, they just hollered, "My land!" Only Joan maintained an aloof silence.

For the first few days of the trip, everyone but Joan had been good-humored and agreeable. No one complained too much about the heat, even though boy, was it hot! Heat rose in waves and made mirages of moisture on the dark tar road as Dad drove west across the panhandle of Florida and all the way to Louisiana, where the sultry air was as thick and heavy as gumbo.

Maryellen's sweaty legs stuck to the plastic seat covers, especially when it was her turn to sit squashed in the middle of the backseat, which everyone had to do except Joan, who insisted on sitting in the front seat next to the window. "I'll get carsick if I ride anywhere else," she announced. Mile after mile she gazed out of the open window at the passing countryside looking very mournful and lovelorn.

"What's the matter with Joan?" asked Beverly in a whisper when they stopped for lunch on the third day.

"I think she just really doesn't want to be on this trip," said Maryellen.

"Yeah," agreed Carolyn. "It seems like the farther away she gets from Jerry, the mopier and moodier she is."

"Well, I don't think it's fair that Joan gets to ride in the front seat with Dad all the time," griped Beverly.

"It's not fair," said Maryellen. "But I don't want to take the risk that she'll be carsick all over everything, do you?"

"No," sighed Beverly.

So, without being challenged, Joan rode in comfort

every day, with a faraway look on her face. *Dreaming of Jerry*, thought Maryellen.

Even though it was crowded in the backseat, the rest of the kids had fun in the car. They sang and played car games like finding all the letters of the alphabet in order on the signs that they passed. Signs for Burma-Shave shaving cream were the best, because they had *u* and *v*, and in the correct order, too. Everyone loved to read aloud the funny poems divided on six separate signs that advertised Burma-Shave, like:

> *She kissed*
> *The hairbrush*
> *By mistake*
> *She thought it was*
> *Her husband Jake*
> *Burma-Shave*

When they got tired of singing or playing the alphabet game, Maryellen, Beverly, and Tom played Sweet 'n' Sour by waving to all the people they passed. Some people were sour and didn't wave, but most people were sweet and smiled and waved back.

The Airstream always attracted and interested people. When the Larkins parked at night at trailer parks or campgrounds, friendly people dropped by to meet the family and to look at the Airstream. When they stopped at roadside attractions, like snake farms and trees so big that you could walk through arches carved in their trunks, the Airstream became a roadside attraction of its own. At gas stations, Dad relied on Maryellen to keep an eye on how many gallons they were buying while he chatted to people about the Airstream. Gas usually cost about 25 cents a gallon, and Maryellen—who loved to do math in her head— soon became fast at figuring out how much money they needed to pay.

One night after dinner, Maryellen was sitting on a rock by the fire with Scooter at her feet and her sketchbook in her lap. Joan was next to her, reading by firelight, but it was as if she were a million miles away, she was so absorbed in her book.

Carolyn appeared, added a log to the fire, and then asked, "What are you drawing, Ellie?"

"The sparks," she answered.

"How come?" asked Carolyn.

"I'm sketching everything I see that flies up—even smoke!" Maryellen explained. "I'm looking for inspiration for the science contest, and Mom says you have to be on the lookout for it all the time."

"Can I see?" asked Carolyn.

"Sure," said Maryellen. She scooted over so that Carolyn could share the rock and look at her sketches.

"Airplanes, birds, bees, leaves, clouds, bubbles, kites, and boomerangs," said Carolyn as she studied the pages. "You've sketched just about everything that goes up in the air."

"Yup," said Maryellen. "I want to show those Sixth-Grade Launchmen boys, especially that bossy Skip, that girls have good ideas, too."

Suddenly Joan looked up. She surprised Maryellen and Carolyn by saying, "Emily Dickinson has a poem that begins, 'Hope is the thing with feathers.'"

Carolyn smiled at Maryellen. "So keep your hopes flying high!"

"I'll try," said Maryellen. She turned to Joan. "I guess you hope this trip will be over soon so you can get back home and marry Jerry."

A funny look—wistful and unsure—slipped across

Joan's face. But then she looked down at her book again. "Mmm," was all she said.

✳

Mom and Dad were very democratic leaders, so everyone in the family had an equal vote on where they should stop and what attractions they'd visit. When Maryellen said they should visit the Alamo, Beverly, Tom, Mikey, and good-natured Carolyn went along. Joan groaned, but she was outvoted.

The Larkins would always remember the Alamo, because that's where tempers began to get short and Dad's idea of togetherness turned into falling-apart-ness for Joan and Maryellen. The day started out badly, even before breakfast, when Joan stayed too long in the bathroom.

"Hurry up," ordered Maryellen as she banged on the bathroom door. "What's taking so long?"

"I'm washing my hair," said Joan crossly from within.

"Again?" wailed Maryellen.

"Go away," shouted Joan.

"Mom," howled Maryellen, "Joan's hogging the bathroom and using up all the hot water—as usual."

"Settle it yourselves," said Mom, just as Mikey knocked over a box of cereal and Scooter began to slurp it up.

When they got to the Alamo, Joan separated herself from the rest of the family and walked around the fort alone. Maryellen and Carolyn saw her from afar, sitting in a sunny corner with her face tilted up to the sun.

"Joan's probably thinking, 'Get me out of here!'" said Maryellen, putting on a crabby voice as she pretended to be Joan. "'This Alamo place is a dump. It smells dank and awful, like steamed broccoli.'"

"Right," Carolyn snickered. "She's thinking that she'll have to wash her hair again—to get the broccoli smell out."

But Maryellen loved the Alamo. When Joan came near, Maryellen ignored her and said to Carolyn, "Gosh, it gives me goose bumps to be where such a famous person as Davy Crockett actually was. Maybe he touched this very wall, or walked this very walkway, or slept in this very room where we are right now." Maryellen bent down and picked up a pebble as a souvenir. "Maybe he stepped on this very rock." She had a sudden, wonderful thought. "Maybe, if I become as famous as Davy Crockett, people will come tour *our* house sometime in the future."

"Maybe!" said Carolyn cheerfully. "Whaddya think, Joan?"

Joan looked thoughtful, and then she said briskly, "I think I'm going to the gift shop to buy a postcard to send to Jerry."

Carolyn and Maryellen rolled their eyes at each other. "It's as if she's not really on this trip with the rest of us at all," said Maryellen.

Relations between Maryellen and Joan were no better when they returned to the Airstream. Maryellen was conscientiously trying to do her job of caring for Scooter. Tonight, like every night, as Mom tried to teach Joan how to prepare dinner, Maryellen filled Scooter's dog-food bowl and then sang the Chow-Chow Dog Food jingle to call Scooter to dinner. The jingle went to the tune of "Twinkle, Twinkle, Little Star." Maryellen sang:

> *Chow-Chow Dog Food,*
> *Eat it up,*
> *And you'll be a*
> *Happy pup!*

"You're driving me crazy with that song," Joan complained to Maryellen, looking up from scouring a pan she'd burned. "It's stuck in my head!"

"Sor-ree!" said Maryellen. But she wasn't, really. She and Scooter liked the song. In fact, Maryellen made a point of humming the tune as Scooter ate his dinner.

✳

After the Alamo, the Larkins drove west and north. They had three rainy days in a row when it was so wet that no one could sleep in the tent or in sleeping bags outside under the stars—and anyway, there were no stars—so they all had to cram inside the Airstream. The little boys slept in the bedroom with Mom and Dad, and the four girls slept in the living room. There were only two couches, so Carolyn, Maryellen, and Beverly took turns sleeping on the floor while Joan slept on one of the couches every night, uncontested.

Even though it was crowded, Maryellen loved the nights when everyone was in the Airstream. She thought it felt cozy and sweet, the way it must have felt to sleep in a covered wagon like the ones on her TV

Westerns, or a snowed-in log cabin in Davy Crockett's Tennessee mountains.

But after the third day of rain, Mom put her foot down and insisted that they stop at a motel. The kids flopped on the beds and watched TV while Dad cleaned the inside of the car. Mom went to the Laundromat to wash and dry the wet towels that had festooned the Airstream's living room, draped like dripping curtains everywhere. Then Mom made a quick run to a supermarket to buy dog food for Scooter and TV dinners for the rest of the family, which she cooked in the Airstream kitchen. All the kids enjoyed eating from the divided trays. Best of all, they could throw the trays away, so there were no dishes to wash.

Still, Maryellen was glad when they were back on the road again. Sitting in the backseat of the car, she rolled down the window and let the wind whip her hair around as she admired the view. She thought back to school, with Mrs. Humphrey at the piano leading the class in a rousing rendition of "America the Beautiful." Maryellen always sang nice and loud, belting out the lyrics with as much gusto as the rest of the class put together:

O beautiful for spacious skies,
For amber waves of grain,
For purple mountain majesties
Above the fruited plain!

But it wasn't until now, driving across America with her family, that Maryellen really understood what the words meant. The skies above Nebraska truly were spacious, and the vast fields of grain in Kansas really did look like golden waves in a windswept ocean. It gave her a thrill to see that the mountains in Wyoming were purple as they rose up against the horizon.

Joan might be longing for home, but Maryellen wasn't. She loved seeing the country with her own eyes. *Yes*, she thought, *America **is** beautiful*.

✳

"Now, kids," said Dad when they got to Yellowstone National Park, "you are about to see one of the wonders of the world. It's a geyser called Old Faithful. Stand back and pay attention."

At first, nothing happened. Then, from a hole in the ground, water and steam burbled up. Next, water sprayed up like a fountain, until—*whoosh!*—the geyser shot up into the air as tall as a skyscraper in a spectacular explosion of scalding hot water, spray, and steam that shook the earth beneath their feet.

"*Whoa!*" gasped Maryellen and Beverly, clutching each other as the crowd applauded the geyser.

Maryellen tilted her head back to see the top of the geyser against the blue sky. *If a geyser of water was lifting something and holding it aloft, would that count as a flying machine?* She gazed at it in wonder as the shaft erupted in a column for nearly five minutes and then sank lower, lower, lower, until it disappeared, hissing, back into the ground.

"Let's see it again!" said Tom, to show how much braver he was than Mikey, who was hiding behind Mom.

"We'll have to wait about an hour," said Dad. "It erupts every sixty-four minutes or so. That's why they call it Old Faithful." So the kids played tag and chased one another around the geyser basin until it was time for Old Faithful to erupt again. This time, Dad lined them up and asked a ranger to take a family photo that made it look as if Old Faithful was shooting up out of Mom's head. Even Joan loosened up and joined in the fun, pretending to be washing her hair. Everyone thought that was hilarious.

Maryellen was glad to see Mom laugh. Mom had not looked very relaxed since they'd left home. It was easy to see why: The family was not exactly being Old Faithful about doing the chores and keeping the promises they had made to Mom.

After the geyser erupted one more time, Dad unhitched the Airstream and drove the station wagon around Grand Loop Road so that everyone could see elk, buffalo, and bears. They hiked to the Grand Canyon of the Yellowstone, and they walked near the hot springs that burbled up out of the ground, holding their noses to block the sulfurous smell. But when they returned to the Airstream, Maryellen noticed that Mom had to hurry and make dinner, and after dinner, when the rest of the family went to hear a ranger talk about stargazing, Mom stayed at the campground to put Mikey to bed and tidy up the trailer.

Mom didn't grumble about it, but Maryellen could see that Mom's prediction had come true: The trip was hard work for her. Tom and Mikey were just mess machines and too young to clean up or help. Beverly was slapdash at setting the table, and Carolyn was unreliable about taking out the trash.

And Joan? Well, Mom was trying to teach Joan how to cook, and Joan was trying to learn so that she'd know how to cook for Jerry after they were married. But Joan's cooking apprenticeship wasn't going very well. Everything that Joan cooked turned out the same way: burned black. Hamburgers, cookies, pancakes, baked potatoes, and fried eggs all became hockey pucks because Joan would get so distracted by whatever book she was reading that she'd forget what she was cooking until smoke filled the Airstream. It got so that whenever anyone smelled smoke, the first thing he or she hollered was "Joan!"

"Joan could burn water," Maryellen muttered to Carolyn when faced with one particularly pitiful grilled cheese sandwich that looked like a lump of charcoal.

As a result of Joan's food flare-ups, Mom had to be vigilantly on cooking duty most nights.

Even Dad was sort of letting Mom down. Fish turned out to be harder to catch than Dad had expected, so Mom had to come up with something for dinner even after long days of hiking, which meant that both Mom and Dad were disappointed.

Maryellen tried to be very conscientious and keep her promise about caring for Scooter. She walked Scooter around the campground every morning. Even though it was a chore, it was fun. Everyone was friendly, and everyone loved Scooter, who had very good manners for a dog. Maryellen enjoyed meeting the people in the campground, who came from all over. They cooked different foods, spoke with different accents, and sang different songs from the ones she knew. There was even a family at the campground who spoke Italian, so she used some of the Italian words, like *grazie* and *ciao*, that Angela had taught her.

Of course, Maryellen had some disappointments, too. One was horseback riding.

When Dad announced, "Today is the Fourth of July, and I have a special day planned!" Maryellen had looked up from her sketchbook with anticipation.

"We're all going horseback riding," Dad went on. "I bought everybody a cowboy hat and a bandanna. So get ready, cowpokes!"

"Yahoo!" cheered the kids as they put on their hats and knotted their bandannas around their necks. They grinned at one another, saying, "Howdy, pardner! Giddyup!" and singing the song from *The Roy Rogers Show*:

> *Happy trails to you,*
> *Until we meet again*
> *Happy trails to you*
> *Keep smiling until then.*

Joan and Mom opted out of horseback riding, but Maryellen couldn't wait. She had spent many hundreds of hours watching cowboys ride horses on TV. Now, as Dad led them to the stables, she imagined *herself*—at last!—on a sleek and handsome steed, galloping as fast as the wind, like the star of a TV Western show. It was a dream come true!

But when she saw the actual horses in real life, she was a little taken aback. They were awfully big, for one thing. Also, they were smelly. They stamped their heavy feet, swished their tails, swung their heads around, and twitched their skin in an unnerving way,

all to get rid of the flies that buzzed around them in
a cloud.

"I guess I should sketch these flies around my
horse," Maryellen joked to Carolyn.

"I guess I should get my horse a toothbrush,"
Carolyn answered, pointing to her horse's giant yellow
teeth.

On the trail, Maryellen's horse kept bending down
to yank up hunks of grass to eat. He walked as slowly
as Scooter did, and every so often startled her with
loud, ornery snorts. When the ride was over, everyone
was bowlegged, sore-bottomed, sweaty, dusty, smelly,
and very hot and tired.

"Buck up, buckaroos," Dad rallied them. "Because
it's the Fourth of July, there's going to be a barbecue
with music and square dancing at Old Faithful Lodge.
After that, we'll drive outside the park to see some
fireworks!"

"Hurray!" cheered the kids, forgetting all about
feeling tired at the prospect of such fun.

Maryellen cheered the loudest. "I love fireworks,"
she exclaimed.

"I know you do, Ellie, honey, but Scooter does not,"

said Mom. "He is very scared of sudden, loud noises like thunder and firecrackers and fireworks."

"I'll say," said Carolyn. "Remember when he went crazy during that thunderstorm? I've never seen him move so fast."

"Poor Scooter," said Tom, petting him on the head sympathetically.

Mom continued, "So someone has to stay behind in the trailer with Scooter tonight to keep him calm in case anyone sets off firecrackers or fireworks nearby." Mom turned to Maryellen. "And since Scooter is your responsibility, Ellie, I think you are that someone."

"But—" Maryellen started to protest.

Mom held up her hand to stop Maryellen. "You promised, remember?"

Maryellen nodded.

"I'll stay, too," said Joan. "I want to wash my hair and iron a blouse."

"Watch out," Carolyn whispered to Maryellen as she left with the rest of the family. "Don't let Joan fry her blouse as if it's a grilled cheese sandwich."

Maryellen mustered a smile, but she felt like Cinderella stuck at home while everyone else went to the ball, even though in this case it was a square dance. It was hard to sound cheerful as she sang Scooter's come-to-dinner song:

> *Chow-Chow Dog Food,*
> *Eat it up,*
> *And you'll be a*
> *Happy pup!*

"Ellie!" Joan said, sounding testy. "Would you please stop singing that song? It's so annoying. Scooter is, too, the way he slobbers over his dinner."

"Okay, okay!" snapped Maryellen. She gave Scooter an extra helping of dog food and an extra scratch behind his ears to make up for Joan's mean words about him.

When it got dark, Maryellen looked out the windows of the Airstream. She could hear fireworks in the distance, but the windows were too small and the trees were too big for her to see them. She sighed with frustration and boredom. She slid her eyes sideways to look at Scooter, who was snoozing under a bed and so deeply asleep that he looked as though nothing could wake him, not even if a loud firecracker went off right next to him.

Maryellen wandered over and looked out of the screen door. Now she could see some distant explosions high in the sky. Some blossomed like giant chrysanthemums. Others looked like dandelions blown apart by a puff of wind. Others looked like squiggles, or jet streams, or silvery star showers. Some shot straight up, like Old Faithful. Others looked like multicolored snowflakes that dissolved into shiny streams of blue, green, red, and gold as they fell toward earth. Quickly, she popped inside and grabbed her sketchbook and pencil. She hurried back and stood in the doorway, halfway in and halfway out, propping the screen door open with her shoulder.

As she sketched, she noticed that some of the fireworks went off all at once in one tremendous burst, which was lovely, if fleeting. But others went off in stages, climbing higher in the sky. They were spectacular! First there was one explosion, then another explosion higher up than the first, and then a third explosion that was highest of all. Maryellen decided that was her favorite kind. They were wish-come-true fireworks: She wished they wouldn't end, and they *didn't*—at least not until they'd burst three times. Each part boosted the next, and that's why they lasted the longest.

Wait a second, she thought, her heart thumping. *That's it—booster rockets!* Her team should make their flying machine in parts, each part lifting the next part up. That was how to keep it in the air longer!

Maryellen was so excited that she stepped outside, and as if the fireworks were celebrating with her, they lit up the whole sky. Then *rat-a-tat-rat-a-tat-tat!* An incredibly loud string of firecrackers exploded, and *zoom!* Scooter burst out the screen door, bolted past Maryellen, and disappeared into the dark.

Disaster!

CHAPTER NINE

O h no!" wailed Maryellen. "Scooter? Scooter, come back, boy!" She dropped her sketch-book, ran around the outside of the Air-stream, and flung herself onto her stomach on the ground, trying to see if Scooter was lying underneath the trailer as he did when it was hot and sunny. "Scooter, I know you're scared. Come on out, *please*."

But Scooter was gone, swallowed up by the night.

"Ellie, what are you shouting about?" asked Joan, leaning out of the screen door. She had just emerged from the bathroom, dripping wet and wrapped in a towel.

"It's Scooter," said Maryellen in a shaky voice. "He ran off. It's all my fault. I was distracted—think-ing about my flying machine and sketching the fire-works—and I opened the door, and someone set off firecrackers, and Scooter bolted out and took off and—"

"Calm down," interrupted Joan. "Scooter can't have gone far. Just rattle his bag of dog food and call him. He'll come."

"No, he's gone," Maryellen insisted. "Please, Joan, you've got to help me find him before he gets eaten by a bear, or gets sucked into one of those smelly mud pots, or falls over a waterfall."

"Oh, all right," said Joan. "You get the flashlight while I get dressed."

"Thank you, Joan," said Maryellen.

"Go!" said Joan, bossily shooing Maryellen. "Get a map of the park, too."

The light from the flashlight bounced along the pine-needly path as Maryellen and Joan set out to search for Scooter. They went to every tent or trailer in the campground to ask if anyone had seen him. Most people had gone to the party at the Lodge, but those still at the campground all knew and liked Scooter because he was such a friendly dog, and they promised to keep an eye out for him.

One man, who was rather well padded himself, said, "Who'd have thought fat old Scooter could run fast or far? He's such a tub of lard."

Maryellen was surprised and pleased when Joan stiffened and said tartly, "Guess we shouldn't judge by appearances, should we?"

I never thought I'd see the day that Joan stuck up for Scooter, Maryellen thought. *I guess she really does like Scooter after all.*

A young woman by the shower house said that she'd seen Scooter running out of the campground a little while ago.

"Was he going toward the Lodge?" Maryellen asked.

"No, the other way." The young woman pointed off into the darkness. "I hope you find him soon."

"Thanks," said Maryellen. She turned to Joan. "Maybe we should go toward the Lodge. If Mom and Dad are still there, we can tell them that Scooter is lost."

"No," said Joan. "I'm sure they've left to go see the fireworks by now. Anyway, it'll be better to find Scooter than to get them all upset for nothing."

They stood under the light on the corner of the shower house and peered at the map. "Oh no," groaned Maryellen. "Scooter is headed toward the Yellowstone canyon! What if he falls into the Firehole River and gets swept away by the rapids?"

"Stop it," said Joan firmly. "That sort of talk won't help." She tapped the map. "Look. There's a ranger station in that same direction. We'll go tell them our dog is missing. We can look for Scooter on the way there."

"Okay," said Maryellen. At times like this, she was glad that Joan was bossy.

The girls walked in silence for a while, following the small shaft of light that Maryellen's flashlight made on the path. Surrounding them was utter, solid darkness. Suddenly, Joan grabbed her shoulder. "What's that?" she whispered.

"What?" asked Maryellen.

"That panting sound," said Joan. "What if it's a bear or a mountain lion following us?"

"Maybe it's Scooter!" said Maryellen. She swung the light around them but saw nothing. She held her breath and listened, then said, "I think you just heard me breathing hard. But if you're worried about wild animals, we should sing really loud. That will scare them away."

"You're kidding," said Joan. "Where'd you learn *that*?"

"Television," said Maryellen. "Probably on one of

those cowboy shows that I like so much and you *dis*like so much."

Joan laughed. "I know a song we can sing really loud," she said. She began to sing, *"Davy, Davy Crockett . . ."*

And Maryellen joined in: *"King of the wild frontier!"*

After singing a few more television theme songs, Maryellen and Joan sang Christmas carols. Finally, Joan said, "Did we make a wrong turn? I thought we'd see the ranger station by now."

"Me, too," said Maryellen. "Let's go back to that fork in the path."

By now, they were in such deep woods that they couldn't see the sky. Joan led the way, and Maryellen kept the light shining by their feet so that they wouldn't trip over tree roots or rocks in the path. She was just thinking how she wished she'd worn jeans instead of shorts, since low branches were scratching her legs, when she thought she heard a rushing sound like cars on a highway, except of course that there were no cars or highways nearby. *Must be the wind in the trees*, she thought, *or a river.* She gasped. *A river?*

"Hey, Joan," Maryellen said. "Wait a second." But she was too late.

One second Joan was there, walking right in front of her, and the next second Maryellen heard a thump and an anguished scream. Joan had disappeared.

"*Joan!*" shrieked Maryellen.

"Help!" came the muffled reply. "Ellie, help!"

"Where are you?" cried Maryellen, frantically shining the flashlight all around her but seeing only pine trees.

"I don't know," wailed Joan. "I just stepped off into nowhere. I've fallen off the path somehow. Hurry up. But don't do what I did. Be careful!"

Maryellen dropped to her hands and knees and then onto her stomach. She slithered forward like a snake with her arms outstretched, slowly swinging the flashlight in an arc from side to side. She was so scared and shaky that the light from the flashlight was jiggly. Suddenly, she came to a sharp drop-off. The path collapsed into a washout that fell down to the rushing river below.

"I can see your light," called Joan. "I'm down here."

Maryellen tilted the flashlight down, and there was Joan, about six feet down in the darkness. She was holding on to a tree root with one hand and balancing on one foot on a rock that stuck out from the steep hillside. She was too far down for Maryellen to reach with her hands.

"Hang on," said Maryellen. She sat up and pulled off her belt. Quickly, she looped the belt around her ankle, flopped back onto her stomach, wrapped her arms around a stout tree trunk, and inched her way backward so that her legs were hanging over the ledge. "Grab the belt," she ordered.

"Don't be stupid," said Joan, sounding impatient. "First of all, I can't even see the belt because it's pitch black down here. Secondly, I'm too heavy. I'd pull you down here, and then we'd be worse off than ever. Think of something else."

"Okay," said Maryellen. This time, she buckled the belt around the flashlight and dangled it as low over the edge as it could go. "Can you climb toward the light?" she asked.

"Yes, I think so," said Joan, "now that it's kind of lighting the way for me."

Maryellen could hear Joan breathing hard as she scrabbled up the vertical incline using rocks and roots as toeholds and handholds until at last, with an *ooph*,

✳ Disaster! ✳

Joan dragged herself over the lip. Maryellen grabbed Joan by the seat of her pants and hauled her all the way up onto flat ground.

For a second, both girls huffed and panted. Then Joan said, "Thanks, Ellie-kins." Joan stood up, but winced when she put weight on her right foot. "Oh no," she moaned.

"What?" asked Maryellen.

"I think I sprained my ankle in the fall," said Joan. She tested putting weight on her foot again. "*Ow, ow, ow*," she said.

Maryellen yanked off her cowgirl bandanna. With the flashlight, she found two sticks and put one on either side of Joan's ankle as splints. She wrapped her bandanna around the sticks and the ankle and tied the bandanna tightly. Then she found a tall, thick stick with a notch at the top and gave it to Joan. "Here, use this as a crutch," she said.

"Jeez Louise, Ellie," said Joan, almost laughing. "Where'd you learn how to do all this rescue and first aid? Girl Scouts?"

Maryellen shook her head. "On the Davy Crockett show, people are always falling off cliffs or slipping into quicksand and spraining their ankles and stuff. I've always liked pretending I'm Davy, rescuing somebody."

Joan snorted. "Okay, so maybe that guy with the dead raccoon on his head is not so useless after all," she said. She gave Maryellen a little hug with her free arm, and then left it across Maryellen's shoulders to lean on her as they walked.

"We'd better just go back to the campground," said Maryellen. "We can try again to find Scooter when it's light out."

Joan nodded. Maryellen could tell that it took all of her strength to keep going because she tensed with every step.

"Listen, Joan," Maryellen said. "I'm sorry about all this."

"All what?" asked Joan.

Maryellen sighed. "Well, I know that you think Scooter is a pain. And now, because I wasn't paying attention to him, Scooter is lost and you've got a sprained ankle. What a disaster."

"It is a disaster, isn't it?" said Joan. To Maryellen's surprise, she chuckled. "You know what, though? It's weird, but I kind of like it."

"You do?" squeaked Maryellen.

"Yes," said Joan. "It's like an adventure in a book." She squeezed Maryellen's shoulder. "Or a TV show."

"Well, shtick with me, shweetheart," Maryellen joked, trying to sound like Humphrey Bogart in the movies. "I can get you into all the disasters you'd ever want!" Then, turning serious, she asked, "You mean you aren't even sorrier to be on this trip? You don't hate it even more now?"

Joan sighed. "I don't hate this trip," she said.

"Then how come you've been so distracted and moody?" asked Maryellen. "Haven't you been staring out the car window, missing Jerry and wishing you were home?"

"I do miss Jerry," said Joan. "But when I'm staring out the car window, I'm just trying to drink it all in. It's as if every house and town that we pass is a book, and I'm curious about its story. I even found the Alamo interesting. That's why I wanted to walk around it alone."

"Really?" asked Maryellen, amazed. She and Carolyn had completely misunderstood Joan! "If you like the trip, why haven't you said so?"

"Well," said Joan, taking a deep breath, "partly because I didn't want to admit that I was wrong. And partly because I would have felt disloyal to Jerry." She paused, and then said, "Ellie, I'm all mixed up, and I'm afraid I've sort of taken it out on you and Scooter. I'm sorry. See, this trip has made me realize that the world is a great big fascinating place. If I've seemed distracted and moody, it's because I—" Joan wavered, and then she blurted out, "I'm questioning my decision to get married."

Maryellen stopped abruptly. "What?" she gasped.

"I love Jerry," said Joan quickly, "and I love the idea of living with him. Even though so far," she joked, "a fire extinguisher seems to be the kitchen utensil I use the most, so we'll starve if he can't cook."

"That's true," said Maryellen with a chuckle. Then she was serious and asked, "So do you have any idea what you're going to do?"

"Well, yes, I do," said Joan. "And actually, you are the one who gave me the idea."

"I did?" said Maryellen.

"Remember at the Alamo, when you were saying how exciting it was to be where Davy Crockett had really been?" said Joan. "You made me think how I'd love to go to Massachusetts and see where my favorite poet, Emily Dickinson, lived. And I've always wanted to see the home of Louisa May Alcott, who wrote *Little Women*, and see Thoreau's Walden Pond. And then there's New York City. Lots of writers lived there, and London, and Paris . . . I want to travel and visit the places where all the writers that I love have lived. I want to go to college and study the books they've written. And then I'd love to help other people love those books and writers as much as I do, maybe by becoming a teacher."

"Oh," said Maryellen, thinking hard. She and Joan walked in silence for a bit. Finally she asked, "Do you have to choose between Jerry and college? Can't you have both? I mean, you can still go to college if you're married, right? And the same goes for traveling. Maybe Jerry would like to travel, too. Have you ever asked him?"

"No," said Joan slowly. Maryellen couldn't see her, but she could tell by her voice that Joan was smiling as she said, "No, I haven't. But I will. I sure will as soon as we get home." With the arm that was not on the crutch, Joan reached over and hugged Maryellen.

"You have great ideas, Ellie. Thanks."

Just then, a twig snapped in the dark woods beside the path. Maryellen and Joan stopped still and clutched each other.

"Quick, let's sing," said Joan.

"I'm too tired," said Maryellen. "I can't even think of a song."

"I can," said Joan. Her voice was very loud, and only quavered a little as she sang,

> *Chow-Chow Dog Food,*
> *Eat it up,*
> *And you'll be a*
> *Happy pup!*

Rustle, rustle, crack. Something was slithering toward them through the underbrush, coming closer and closer. Joan and Maryellen held their breath, and the wild animal stalking them swaggered out onto the path.

It was Scooter.

Both girls dropped to their knees—Joan very gingerly—and hugged him. "Scooter!" they cried with joy.

❋ Disaster! ❋

"Oh, I am so glad to see you!" said Maryellen.

Joan even kissed Scooter on his nose. "Where have you been?" she chided him. "You scared us to death!"

Scooter remained calm. He acted as if causing more excitement than the Fourth of July fireworks was all in the course of a perfectly normal day for him. He yawned as Joan used her crutch to struggle to her feet, and he graciously allowed Maryellen to carry him all the way back to the campground. After a while, he fell asleep and snored—with gusto—in her arms.

❋

Maryellen, Scooter, and Joan had not been back long before the rest of the Larkins returned from the fireworks.

"All quiet here on the home front?" asked Dad.

Maryellen and Joan lifted their eyebrows at each other. "Not exactly," said Maryellen. "It was all my fault, really," she confessed. "You see—"

But Joan interrupted. "*I'll* tell what happened," she said, in her good old take-charge way.

So Joan told the whole story of Scooter's disappearance, summing it up with, "Ellie is a real hero. She was brave and knew just what to do."

"Does this mean that you will help Ellie take care of Scooter from now on?" asked Mom with a twinkle in her eye.

"Uh, no," said Joan swiftly. "Not entirely, that is. But there's one thing I can do—help her call him to dinner!"

Scooter howled as the whole family sang,

Chow-Chow Dog Food,
Eat it up,
And you'll be a
Happy pup!

Groups

Joan's ankle healed quickly, and all the way home across the country from Wyoming to Florida, she held true to her promise. Every evening, she helped Maryellen summon Scooter to dinner, whistling along in harmony while Maryellen sang the dog-food song. Sometimes, Joan winked at Maryellen while she whistled, in silent acknowledgment of the conversation they'd had in the woods. Maryellen felt grown-up to be the only one who knew Joan's secret hopes and dreams and ambitions. She was pleased to have this special bond with Joan. They even had their own private theme song!

Nevertheless, even Maryellen was pretty tired of the Chow-Chow Dog Food song by the time Dad pulled into their driveway. They all climbed out of the car feeling stiff and sweaty and very glad to be home.

"Home sweet home," Mom sang out. "There's no place like home! Oh, how I've missed the space and peace and privacy of our wonderful house!"

"Welcome back!" said Grandmom, as she gathered Beverly, Tom, and Mikey in a big hug. Grandpop hugged Carolyn and Maryellen.

Jerry was there to greet Joan. He scooped her up in a hug, too, a hug that was only for her. "Did you miss me?" he asked.

"I sure did," said Joan. "Oh, I have so much to tell you!"

Maryellen caught Joan's eye and smiled.

"How was your trip?" Grandpop asked Maryellen. He waved a map in his hand. "Can you show me your route?"

"I'd love to," said Maryellen.

"Did you use the sketchbook that I gave you?" asked Grandmom.

"I sure did," said Maryellen. "I can't wait to show you all the flying things that I sketched."

"I'm glad you're home, dear heart," said Grandmom.

"Me, too," said Maryellen.

"Me, too," said Mom. She put her hands on her hips, tipped her head toward the Airstream, and said to Dad with semi-pretend exasperation, "I'm glad to be here, even if I do have to put up with this gigantic silver spaceship parked in our driveway. I feel as if I'm living at Cape Canaveral."

"Now, honey—" Dad began.

But Grandpop interrupted. "Come on and tell me about all the fish you caught," he said to Dad, and off the two men went.

✳

"I've never been so excited for the first day of school," Maryellen said to Davy a few days later. She skipped a skip of happiness as they walked to school together. Her booster-rocket idea boosted her confidence: She was sure that now the Launchmen would listen to her and be impressed with her brainstorm. "When's the first meeting of the Science Club?"

"Not till next week," said Davy. "Don't worry, you didn't miss much at the summer meetings. Mostly, Skip just talked. We still don't have a good idea for a flying machine."

"I do," said Maryellen. "Well, I have part of an idea."

"What is it?" asked Davy.

But before she could answer, Wayne screeched up from behind them on his bike, the propeller on his beanie hat spinning wildly. He slammed on his brakes to make his bike skid sideways right in front of Maryellen so that she had to stop short. "Watch out, Wayne!" she said.

"Greetings, earthlings," said Wayne in a flat voice like a robot.

Maryellen sighed. *Here we go*, she thought, *starting another school year with zany Wayne.*

Maryellen said to Davy, "I'll tell you my idea later." She didn't want to say anything in front of Wayne because she was sure that he'd blab her idea all over to everyone in the Science Club before she had a chance to present it. It was hard not to tell Davy, though. She felt almost as if she had fireworks with booster rockets going off inside herself. She was positive that good old Davy would share her enthusiasm.

Before classes began, Principal Carey announced over the PA system that the new fourth- and fifth-grade classes should meet in the auditorium. As Maryellen walked down the hallway and found a seat in the auditorium, she couldn't help noticing that no one noticed *her* anymore. No kids stared at her, or pointed her out to one another as "the girl whose picture was in the newspaper." Apparently, her fame had faded away over the summer. *Never mind,* thought Maryellen. She sat up straight, feeling all the more determined to impress everybody all over again, this time as the girl who single-handedly helped the Launchmen win the science contest with her fantastic flying idea.

When the classes were gathered, Principal Carey made a startling announcement. "Our school building is so crowded that it is bursting at the seams," he said. "So to use our space efficiently, and to improve academic performance, we'll now have 'pullout groups.' Some students will be pulled out of their homeroom classrooms and sent to different teachers for math and English."

Everybody knew that meant they were being separated by ability, and the smartest kids would all be in the same pullout groups. As the day went on, the girls found out that Angela, who was a math whiz, and

Maryellen were in the top math group, but the Karens were not. Maryellen and Karen King were in the top English class, but Angela and Karen Stohlman were not.

When the girls met at lunch, Karen King lifted her milk carton to toast Maryellen, saying, "Congratulations on being chosen for both the top pullout groups, Ellie."

"Oh," said Maryellen, "thanks."

Karen Stohlman sighed. "I liked it better when we were all in the same class. Now that we're in different groups, we won't see one another as much as we used to."

"I know," said Angela. "That's too bad."

"Yes," said Karen King. "It's hard to be friends when you hardly ever see each other."

"Let's be together every chance we get, like at lunch and recess," said Angela. "I'm going to be a Girl Scout this year, so we'll be together at meetings. And our new homeroom teacher, Miss Martinez, is starting a baton-twirling club. We could all join that."

"Yes! Good idea!" said the Karens.

Everyone looked at Maryellen. "I don't think I can join anything else new," she said slowly. "I just joined the Science Club."

"Oh," said Angela, crestfallen. "Right."

"What if the Science Club meets at the same time as a group you've been in for a long time, like Girl Scouts?" asked Karen Stohlman. "Which one will you choose?"

"Well, I, uh," Maryellen stumbled over her words. "I'm pretty excited about the contest. I drew lots of sketches over the summer, and I have a really good idea for a flying machine. So, I guess . . . I guess I'd choose the Science Club."

Maryellen's friends were quiet. The silence was awkward, weighted down with hurt feelings. Finally, Karen King, who had a knack for stating things clearly, said, "No offense, Ellie, but it seems like it's more important to you to be in the Science Club than it is to be our friend."

Karen Stohlman didn't chime in, but she didn't disagree. Angela added swiftly and sweetly, "We're not mad, we're just sad."

Maryellen felt terrible. Was it selfish of her to hurt and disappoint her friends? Was she wrong to go off on her own? She balled up the rest of her sandwich and put it back in her lunch bag. Her throat was so tight she knew she couldn't swallow another bite.

"So what are you going to do?" asked Karen King.

"I don't know," said Maryellen.

Even though it was a very hot day, there was a chill in the air.

"Oh, well," said Angela, trying to sound chipper. "At least we have right now to be together. I brought a jump rope. Let's go outside and jump until we have to go to our next class."

Maryellen, relieved not to be the focus of attention anymore, led the way as the four girls tossed their lunch bags in the trash and headed outside to the playground.

Get To It!

CHAPTER ELEVEN

That afternoon, the air was so soupy that it was hard to breathe. So after school, Maryellen and Carolyn walked the little kids down to the beach. Joan was already there, camped out comfortably under a beach umbrella, reading.

"Hi, Joan," they said.

"Hi," she answered, not looking up from her book.

The kids tossed their towels next to Joan and stampeded down the sand and into the water.

Maryellen plunged headfirst under the first giant wave coming toward her and heard it thunder above her and crash behind her onto the shore. She bobbed up, blinking in the glaring sunlight that bounced off the water, and grinned. As usual, the ocean refreshed her. Nobody could feel hot and bothered or grumpy-grouchy-gloomy in the ocean! She could see Carolyn playing with Beverly, Tom, and Mikey, splashing in the shallow water, and she could hear them laughing and shouting with glee as the water tickled their legs.

After a while, Maryellen strolled back up the beach to Joan's umbrella and flopped onto a beach towel.

Joan looked up. "How was your first day of school?"

"Not so good," said Maryellen.

"How come?" asked Joan.

"Well, the Karens and Angela have hurt feelings because I'm staying in the Science Club, which means we won't see each other much," Maryellen explained.

"Why are you staying in the Science Club?" asked Joan. "I thought you said that those sixth-grade boys were annoying."

"They are," sighed Maryellen. "But I just really love the idea of inventing a flying machine."

"Well, I think if you love something, you have to stick to it and stand up for it," said Joan. "If it is right for you, then you should do it. Even if it doesn't make sense to other people, or isn't what they expect you to do. If you love it, do it."

"Is that how you feel about reading?" Maryellen asked.

"Yes. I love reading," said Joan, with a contented sigh. "I love books better than anything."

"Better than Jerry?" asked Maryellen curiously.

Joan replied slowly, "Noooo."

"Is it a tie?" asked Maryellen.

"Mm-hmm," said Joan. She made an apologetic face and nodded. "I'm afraid it is."

"Why're you afraid?" asked Maryellen. "It's not as if you have to choose between Jerry and books. You can have both, can't you? Have you spoken to Jerry about going to college yet?"

"Yes," said Joan. "And he thinks it's a great idea for me to go—someday. But right now, we can't afford it. See, because Jerry was in the Navy in the Korean War, he's been living in the dorm and taking classes free of charge. The G.I. Bill pays for returning veterans to go to college. But married students have to live in married-student housing, and even though the rent is low and Jerry and I will both be working part-time, we can't afford rent and tuition for me."

"If only you could live somewhere for free," said Carolyn, who had joined them under the umbrella and was helping Mikey dry off while Beverly helped

Tom. "You could live in our house, but it'd be awfully crowded. Some of us would have to sleep in the carport."

"Or in the tent we took on our trip," said Beverly.

"Hey," said Maryellen, bursting with a brainstorm. "How about the Airstream? You and Jerry could live in the Airstream!"

"No rent!" crowed Carolyn. "That's brilliant."

"I'd *love* to live in the Airstream!" gushed Beverly, clasping her hands together in delight.

"I want to live in the Airstream, too," said Tom.

"Me, too," said Mikey.

"Just think, Joan," said Maryellen enthusiastically. "You could park the Airstream by the college most of the time, and then if you wanted to travel and Dad wasn't using it, you could hitch it to Jerry's hot rod and off you'd go! You could drive up to Massachusetts to see where those authors you like lived."

Joan's face brightened with hope momentarily, but then she shook her head. "No, no," she said, sounding sadly practical. "It's cute of you to come up with such a wild idea. But it would never work. For one thing, remember what Mom said? The Airstream is a Very Expensive Thing. What if Mom and Dad want to sell it?"

"Are you kidding?" said Maryellen. "Dad doesn't want to sell it. Mom'll be thrilled to get the Airstream—the 'gigantic silver spaceship' as she calls it—out of the driveway, and Dad'll be thrilled that she's thrilled. You'll be doing both of them a favor."

"Even if that's true, it's still too much to ask Mom and Dad to let Jerry and me take over the Airstream," said Joan, "especially with all the expenses of the wedding coming up." She sighed a sigh from the bottom of her heart. "Mom's turned *that* into a Very Expensive Thing, even though Jerry and I don't want a big hoopla. But Mom's mailing the invitations tomorrow. After that, there'll be no turning back."

"You did give Mom permission to go full speed ahead," said Maryellen.

"I know," Joan admitted unhappily. "But I didn't think she'd go so full speed so far ahead in such a different direction from what Jerry and I want."

"What do you want?" asked Beverly simply.

"You mean besides not making Mom unhappy?" asked Joan.

"Yes," said the other girls.

"Really, truly," said Maryellen.

Joan spoke earnestly. "Really, truly, I'd like to be married right in our backyard, with just our families around us. Nothing big, nothing fancy, nothing to distract us from the most important thing, which is Jerry and me promising to love each other and take care of each other forever." She smiled. "Then we'd celebrate with a little party."

"Cake," said Mikey happily. Though he was young, he knew what was important at a party.

"Oh, right, Mikey honey," said Joan, giving him a swift hug. "Of course! Maybe cupcakes and ice cream cones and lemonade, too."

Maryellen stood up and brushed the sand off her knees. "Okay, then," she said briskly. "Let's get to it."

"Get to what?" asked Joan.

"Your wedding," said Maryellen. "Saturday's the day after tomorrow. I think we can have everything ready by then."

"No, we—I mean, but . . ." Joan spluttered. "A surprise backyard wedding? I just couldn't do that to Mom. She'd be so disappointed! She has her heart set on what she thinks of as a perfect wedding."

"Mom's Mom," said Carolyn, "not a mean

old tyrant. She just wants you to be happy. She'll understand."

"Besides, Mom has five other children," Beverly pointed out. "So she has lots more chances at perfect weddings."

"And didn't you just tell me that if you really love something, you have to stick to it and stand up for it?" said Maryellen. "Didn't you just say that if something is right for you, then you should do it even if it doesn't make sense to other people?"

"Yes, but—" Joan began.

"So your wedding won't be the way other people do it," Maryellen continued. "It'll be the way you and Jerry do it. It'll be perfect for you."

"I guess so," said Joan, a bit dazed.

"Do we still get to wear our bridesmaid dresses?" asked Beverly.

"Of course," said Joan.

"And your bride outfit is ready, all except the veil," said Carolyn.

"You can wear my crown that Ellie made me last Christmas," Queen Beverly offered graciously.

"Or a tutu on your head, like Wayne did after Ellie's

show," joked Carolyn.

"I was thinking maybe just a flower," laughed Joan. She looked at them all and smiled exuberantly. "You know what? Nobody ever had better brothers and sisters than I do. You're helping me make my hopes come true. Thanks a million, you guys!"

✳

On her wedding day, Joan wore a cream-colored gardenia tucked behind her ear. Afterward, everyone agreed that Joan was the most beautiful bride they'd ever seen and that Joan and Jerry's wedding was the most beautiful—and *relaxed*—wedding they'd ever been to. Jerry and the minister stood under the big tree in the Larkins' backyard, and Beverly, Maryellen, and Carolyn—wearing their glamorous bridesmaid dresses, finished by Mrs. Fenstermacher and Grandmom—walked toward them down a pathway lined on either side with buckets of jasmine and hibiscus.

Carolyn had been right, of course: Mom wasn't a tyrant. She had listened to what Joan wanted, and then both she and Joan made compromises. For example, Mom gave in on having a string quartet because Joan thought that was too fancy. Tom had volunteered to sing, *"Here comes the bride, All dressed in white, Stepped on a turtle and down fell her girdle,"* but in the actual ceremony, Carolyn played her piano, softly and sweetly, inside the house. The music was gentle and lovely, wafting through the open door on the balmy breeze as Joan and Dad—and Mom, too, at Joan's insistence— walked toward Jerry and the minister, who stood with dappled sunshine beaming down on them. Maryellen thought that Jerry looked movie-star handsome in his dress-white Navy uniform, and he didn't look at all stiff or formal; he had a smile a mile wide!

After the ceremony, all the guests were given white balloons, white kites, white paper fans, and white tissue-paper flowers. They ate cake (Mom insisted on making a traditional multilayered cake) and ice cream cones (Joan's idea) and strawberries on toothpicks. The kids flew their kites, running around the backyard laughing—watched, but not chased, by Scooter, who snoozed in the shade. Mikey soon fell asleep with frosting on his face. Beverly and Tom got a big kick out of blowing up the extra balloons and then letting them go so that they spiraled around crazily, making a wonderfully rude noise as they deflated: *Pfffft*. Grandmom and Grandpop sat on the patio with Mom and Dad and Jerry's parents, who had driven down from St. Augustine. They fanned themselves with their paper fans and drank lemonade.

"This," sighed Joan to Maryellen as they surveyed the sunny scene, "is exactly what I wanted." Just then, a deflating balloon *pffffte*d its way over to the patio and landed in Dad's lemonade, and Joan and Maryellen laughed.

Joan and Jerry drove off in Jerry's hot rod, trailing the Airstream behind them. Their honeymoon was only going to be the rest of the weekend, because Joan had an interview on Monday with the college admissions office to see if she could enroll in January. But even though the honeymoon was going to be short, Maryellen, Carolyn, and Beverly had thoroughly decorated the back of the Airstream anyway, with a big sign that read, "JUST MARRIED," and a string of old shoes and tin cans tied to the bumper.

"Good-bye, good-bye," everyone called, and Joan and Jerry drove off in a shower of flower petals.

Dad put his arm around Mom, who was sniffling.

"Aw, sweetheart," Dad said comfortingly, "don't be sad. Kids grow up. That's just what they do."

"I'm not sad," Mom said. "I'm crying tears of joy because I'm just so glad to get that spaceship out of the driveway!"

But as Mom swiped her eyes with a hankie, Maryellen could tell that was only half true. She understood. Her own heart was happy for Joan, but sad at the thought of what it would be like without Joan in the house. There would be an empty space in their family. Even though Joan and Jerry would be nearby, and visit often, nothing would ever be quite the same again.

Maryellen
Takes Off

T he very next day, Florida's September rainy season began with grim determination. The rain was so steady and hard, the downpour seemed almost solid.

"Thank goodness it didn't rain like this yesterday," said Mom. "We'd have had to move the wedding into the carport." As it was, in a dry corner of the carport there were leftovers from the wedding—grounded kites, un-blown-up balloons, crumpled fans, a partly used box of toothpicks, and drooping tissue-paper flowers—that had been hastily tossed into a box. No one had the heart to throw them away.

They were still there the next morning when Davy stopped by to walk to school with Maryellen in the pouring rain.

"I wish I didn't have to go to school today," said

Maryellen, pulling on her boots.

"Because of the rain?" asked Davy.

"No, because I'm nervous about seeing the Karens and Angela," Maryellen explained. "We had sort of a disagreement last week." Normally, Maryellen would be dying to race to school to tell her friends all about Joan's wedding. But today, she wished she had a fiery fever or lumpish mumps or a raging red rash so that Mom would have to let her stay home. Unfortunately, she was in tip-top shape except for a sloshy feeling of dread in her stomach about seeing her friends. After their difficult conversation on Thursday, they had avoided one another on Friday. Would they still be upset? Maryellen wondered now. She opened her umbrella and leaned into the wet, gusty wind. She would just have to see.

Because it was raining, the students gathered in the gym before school started rather than outside on the playground as usual. It was hot in the gym. Maryellen unbuttoned her raincoat and flapped the two sides to cool herself off.

"Good idea," said Angela, appearing at her side with the two Karens.

"Yeah," said Karen King. "I feel like a steamed lobster."

The girls smiled at one another a little sheepishly, and finally Karen Stohlman said, "Listen, Ellie, we're sorry for being so snippy last week."

"Yes," said Angela. "Especially if we're not going to see each other very much, we need to be nice to each other when we do, right?"

"Right," said the Karens and Maryellen.

"Hey," said Angela. "I hear your sister had a surprise wedding on Saturday."

"She did!" said Maryellen. "In our backyard."

"Oh, I think that is the most romantic idea I ever heard," said Karen Stohlman. "I'm going to do that when I get married, too."

"Tell us everything," begged Karen King.

By the time Maryellen had described the wedding in detail, it was time for school to begin. The girls went their separate ways to their separate classes. As she waved good-bye to her friends, Maryellen was so relieved they'd settled their differences so unfussily that, to make them laugh, she began to dance around with her umbrella and sing "Singin' in the Rain," a song from one of her favorite Debbie Reynolds movies.

Later, when they met for lunch, it was only the teeniest bit awkward as the Karens and Angela talked about their Girl Scout meeting to be held that afternoon after school.

"Did you forget to wear your Girl Scout uniform, Ellie?" Karen King asked. Angela jabbed her and frowned. "Oh. Oh, *right*," Karen said quickly. "Your Science Club meets today. I forgot. Well, uh, that'll be fun."

"I hope so," said Maryellen. "Anyway, thanks for not being upset with me anymore about it."

"Well," said Karen Stohlman philosophically, "we're in the fifth grade now. We're more mature than we were in fourth grade, so we're smarter about how dumb it is to fight."

"Yeah," said Karen King. "Plus, we get it that all of us like to do different things. But as long as we still like each other, that's all that matters, right?"

"Right!" agreed the four girls, Maryellen most heartily of all.

✷

Maryellen immediately saw that Davy was correct: She hadn't missed much by not being at the Science Club meetings over the summer, except for the fact that the two other girls had dropped out. As soon as the Sixth-Grade Launchmen were gathered after school in Mr. Hagopian's room, they all began talking at once, launching their ideas forcefully at one another as if the ideas were ballistic missiles. Mr. Hagopian glanced over, but he was too busy with another team to ask the Launchmen to settle down.

"Hey!" said Maryellen to her teammates.

Everyone ignored her.

Maryellen smacked the desk with her sketchbook. "HEY!" she said again. This time everyone stopped talking and looked at her. "The contest is in two weeks. Don't you think we'd better get a plan?"

"We've got a plan," said Skip, full of swagger. "My plan." He spread a crinkly piece of paper on the desk. It was covered with smudged sketches.

"Well, even if your plan is good," said Davy, "we should look at other people's, too."

"Davy's right," said Maryellen. "We should discuss everybody's ideas."

"Nope. Waste of time," said Skip.

"You can't just boss and bully us into using your plan, Skip," said Maryellen. She thought about how Mom and Joan had listened to each other with respect and made compromises so that the wedding pleased them both. "Maybe the best idea will be a combination of lots of different people's ideas."

But unlike Mom, Skip was a tyrant. "Who asked you?" he said.

Maryellen flushed. "I'm a member of the team," she said.

"Oh, yeah? You never came to the summer meetings. We should disqualify you for that, girlie," said one of Skip's buddies.

"It's not in the rules that you have to come to every meeting," said Maryellen. "The rules—"

"Talk all you want to," Skip interrupted. "But we've got the plan for the fastest flying machine right here." He smoothed the paper with his plan on it.

Even at a quick glance, Maryellen could see that Skip's flying machine flew parallel to the ground along a guiding string between two posts. It looked like a pretty standard balsa-wood airplane powered by a wound-up rubber band that spun a propeller like the one on Wayne's beanie.

"Let's just build this and stop whining about the rules," urged a tall boy.

"Have you even read the rules?" asked Maryellen, pulling the paper with the rules on it out of her sketch-book. "If you had, you'd know the contest isn't a race. It isn't about speed; it's about time. The flying machine that stays up in the air the longest wins."

All the Sixth-Grade Launchmen—except Davy and Maryellen—stared at the paper in Maryellen's hands. Then they frowned and mumbled unhappily.

"I tried to tell you guys during the summer," said Davy, "but you wouldn't listen."

"Give me that," ordered Skip, reaching for the rules. After he looked at them, he tossed the paper back to Maryellen and crossed his arms over his chest, saying, "So, what's your idea, genius?"

Everyone turned to look at Maryellen. Except for Davy, they all had expressions of distrust and doubt on their faces.

"Look," she said. She held up her sketchbook to show the Launchmen the sketches she had made of fireworks. "When I was on vacation, I saw fireworks, and I noticed that the fireworks that stayed up in the sky the longest went off in stages. Each explosion lifted the next part higher. So my idea is to use booster rockets to lift the different parts of our flying machine."

"How will the parts connect?" asked one boy.

"Well, I don't know," said Maryellen. "But—"

"How'll they blast off from each other? How'll they know when to blast off from each other?" asked another boy.

"I don't know," said Maryellen again, "I—

"What'll provide the power to make any of it fly up in the first place?" asked another boy.

"I'm not sure yet," said Maryellen. "I thought the whole idea was for us to figure stuff out together, as a team. But I was thinking maybe it could be powered by water. You know, like water out of a squirt gun."

"A squirt gun?" several kids repeated with scornful disbelief. Others howled with laughter, as if she had said something hilariously stupid.

Skip puffed out his lower lip and exhaled with exasperation. "First of all, shooting something up with water will never work," he said, counting off on his fingers. "Second, your whole stages and boosters idea stinks. Third, we don't need a dumb fourth-grade girl to tell us what to do. Got it?"

Maryellen felt a blazing red-hot flash of fury shoot up her spine. She remembered how Mom had left her job at the aircraft factory because her ideas were not respected, and she remembered how Joan had said that you have to stand up for what you love. *That's true flipped around, too,* Maryellen thought. *Sometimes you have to stand up against what you hate.*

She quietly shut her sketchbook and, without saying a word, gathered her belongings to leave. As she stood up, so did Davy.

"Hey, Skip," said Davy. He counted off on his fingers. "First of all, you're a bully. Second, Ellie's idea of stages doesn't stink. Third, we're in the *fifth* grade, and we don't need a stuck-up sixth-grade boy to tell us what to do. Got it?"

"Yeah!" said Wayne. He flicked the propeller on his beanie to make it spin, and then he and Davy followed Maryellen out the door.

The Flying Friends

CHAPTER THIRTEEN

S o did you pitch a big fit and yell like you did when you quit your birthday-party polio show?" asked Karen King. It was still raining, so the girls were in the gym the next morning, waiting for classes to begin. Maryellen had told her friends how she and Davy and Wayne were no longer Launchmen. "Did you storm out of Mr. Hagopian's classroom and slam the door behind you?"

"No," said Maryellen, blushing a little. She felt embarrassed recalling the temper tantrum she'd thrown when she quit the polio show. She had learned from that experience that it's better to stand up for yourself without making a spectacle of yourself. "Davy and Wayne spoke up, but I quit quietly."

"You changed your mind about quitting the polio show," said Angela. "Do you think you might change your mind this time, too, and go back to the Launchmen?"

"No," said Maryellen again. She remembered how the older boys had laughed at her and how Skip had dismissed her for being younger—and a girl.

"You were so excited about planning your flying machine," said Karen Stohlman kindly. "You drew all those sketches in your sketchbook. It's a shame to waste all that work. Does it say in the rules that you have to be on a team? I mean, couldn't you make a flying machine and enter it in the contest by yourself?"

"Fly solo," Karen King piped up.

"I don't think it's against the rules," said Maryellen. "But I also don't think I can make the flying machine all by myself. I need help. I don't even have a complete idea yet. And then I'd also need help to fly the machine at the contest."

"We'll help you," said Angela immediately.

"Really?" asked Maryellen.

"Sure!" said Karen King. "Even if we're not all that interested in flying machines, you're our friend and you want this, so we do, too. The four of us will make our own new team."

"And I bet Davy will help us if we ask him," said Karen Stohlman.

"We should ask Wayne, too," said Maryellen. "After all, he stood up for me."

"Way-ay-ay-ne," sighed Karen Stohlman. The four girls rolled their eyes at one another at the thought of working with Wayne.

"We're trying to make something that'll fly, right?" said Maryellen, feeling happy and lighthearted. "So maybe it'll be useful to have Wayne on our team. He's a birdbrain! Get it?"

The girls giggled and flapped their arms like pretend wings as they parted and headed off to class.

At lunch, Karen Stohlman reported that she had asked Mr. Hagopian if they could form a new team and still enter the contest, and Mr. Hagopian had said it was fine. Maryellen reported that she had invited Davy and Wayne to join the team, and the boys had said yes right away.

"We could call our team the Shooting Stars," suggested Karen King.

"Or the Flying Angels," suggested Angela. "Or the Fine Feathered Flying Friends."

"Or the Straighten Up and Fly Rights," said
Maryellen. That was the name of one of Mom and
Dad's favorite songs by the singer Nat King Cole.

"How about the Fifth-Grade Fliers?" said Karen
Stohlman.

"All these names are good," said Maryellen, who
was determined to be the exact opposite of Skip as a
leader and to respect everyone's ideas. "But if we don't
have a favorite yet, maybe we should wait and see if we
can think of something better. Maybe we'll get an idea
when we see how our machine looks. Okay?"

"Okay," agreed the girls.

So it was a nameless team that met in the Larkins'
carport on Saturday afternoon. Naturally, Mikey, Tom,
Beverly, and Scooter came out to see what was going
on. Scooter went to sleep, and the little kids quickly lost
interest in the team's conversation and began scroung-
ing around in the box of wedding leftovers. Mikey,
who was under the impression that they were having
another wedding, handed everyone either a tissue-
paper flower, or a kite, or a fan. Beverly and Tom found
a bag of balloons. They blew them up and then let them
go to careen around wildly and make the same rude

noise they'd made at Joan's wedding: *Pfffft.*

Wayne was enchanted. He ditched the team meeting to join Beverly and Tom. Since Wayne was bigger than they were, he could blow his balloon up so that it was bigger and flew longer. The rude noise Wayne's balloons made was louder and even more disgusting than Beverly's and Tom's, especially when he used one of the long, hot-dog-shaped balloons.

When one of Wayne's *pfffft*ing balloons smacked Karen Stohlman in the forehead, she said, "Cut it out, Wayne."

But Maryellen smacked her own forehead with the palm of her hand. "That's it—a balloon! Air squirting out of a deflating balloon will provide the power to lift our flying machine."

Davy looked at the kite and the tissue-paper flower Mikey had given him. "I wonder if we could make a tiny little kite out of tissue paper and toothpicks," he mused, "and attach it to the balloon."

"And after the balloon loses all its air, the kite will still fly for a while," said Karen Stohlman, "so our machine will stay up longer."

"Well," said Karen King, who never let enthusiasm

get in the way of constructive criticism, "I don't think one balloon will have enough power to lift even a little kite very high."

Everyone had to admit that this was probably true.

"How about more than one balloon, then?" asked Angela. "How about two?"

"Good idea," said Maryellen, fanning herself with the paper fan Mikey had given her. The fan was made of folded paper held together at the bottom by a rubber band.

Wayne surprised everyone by speaking up. "I still really like Ellie's idea of booster rockets," he said.

"Thanks, Wayne," said Maryellen. She sketched as she talked. "So, okay, what if we blow up three balloons. We attach the kite to the middle balloon. We clip the side balloons shut, and use a rubber band to shut the middle balloon and connect it to the side balloons. When we're ready to launch, we unclip the two side balloons and they take off. When they deflate, the rubber band falls off, so the middle balloon takes off. When it starts to descend, the kite will slow its fall, like a parachute would."

Everyone crowded together to look at Maryellen's

sketch. For a while, no one said anything, and she held her breath in nervousness and hope.

Finally, Davy said slowly, "I get it. The side balloons are the first stage, the middle balloon is the second stage, and the kite is the third stage, even though all it does is glide. Let's try it."

"Good job, Ellie," said Karen Stohlman, nudging Maryellen with her elbow.

"Oh," said Maryellen, "I may have drawn the sketches, but everybody supplied the ideas. Our whole team did a good job."

"We are a good team," said Karen King. "We really should have a name."

"How about the Loony Balloonies?" suggested Davy.

"That's it!" said the Karens and Angela and Wayne—who celebrated by sending another balloon *pffff*ting around the carport.

✳

"My lips are dead," moaned Karen Stohlman. "I think I must have blown up a million balloons."

"Wayne, if you shoot one more rubber band at me,

I'll use it to handcuff your hands together," snapped Karen King.

Wayne stuck two toothpicks in his mouth as if they were fangs and howled like a wolf.

It was a week later, and the Loony Balloonies were gathered again in the Larkins' carport. They had soon realized that a plan on paper and an actual flying machine that really flew in real life were two very different things. Sometimes the balloons popped. Sometimes the kite fell off. Sometimes the rubber band was too tight. Sometimes the clips were too loose.

They worked all afternoon. Angela was endlessly patient about gluing the tissue paper onto the toothpicks to make the tiny kites, and Davy was best at attaching them to the balloons. Even though she complained, Karen Stohlman blew up balloon after balloon after balloon. Karen King was really good at spotting problems and tireless about pointing out mistakes. When they needed metal clips and glue, Wayne sped off on his bike and fetched them quickly. And just when everyone was so tired and discouraged that they were about to quit and go home in defeat, Maryellen cheered them up and made them laugh by tossing scraps of white tissue paper into the air and pretending it was snow.

Now it was practically dinnertime, and at last, the team finally felt sure they had figured out how to construct a three-stage, balloon-powered, tissue-paper-kite flying machine that worked reliably. The floor of the carport was strewn with balloons and broken toothpicks. Bits of white tissue paper lay scattered all over. But after hours and hours of experimenting and improving and trying again and again, the team was prepared for the contest, which was taking place the next Saturday.

"I think we're ready," said Maryellen optimistically.

"Well, we're as ready as we'll ever be," said Karen King. "It'll either fly or it won't."

No one could contradict that statement, even if it wasn't the most uplifting thought in the world.

The Most
Important Thing

he day of the science contest was bright and
clear. The playground was spongy underfoot
from all the rain, but the sky above was blue.
The Loony Balloonies stood in a silent cluster, looking
at all the other teams lining up on the field preparing
their very impressive flying machines. Davy spoke for
the whole team when he said with genuine concern,
"Wow."

"Yeah," said Karen King. "I didn't realize we'd be
competing against rocket ships. Some of these gizmos
look like they could fly to the moon, for Pete's sake."

"Come on," said Maryellen briskly. "Let's get
ready." She led her friends to set themselves up as far
away from the Sixth-Grade Launchmen as possible—
all the way across the playground. Even so, from that
distance, Maryellen and her team could see and hear

the Launchmen bickering as usual, all talking at once and no one listening to what anyone else had to say. It cheered the Loony Balloonies up tremendously to see that the Launchmen were still such a disorganized mess of a team, and they set to work preparing their balloons with renewed enthusiasm.

"Our machine may not work better than theirs," said Angela. "But our team sure does."

Angela turned out to be wrong. The balloon-powered, tissue-paper-kite flying machine worked *better* than the Launchmen's rubber-band-propelled plane. When Davy took the clips off, the two booster balloons effortlessly lifted the middle balloon high into the sky.

Maryellen tilted her head back and shaded her eyes. She felt as if her heart was flying up, too. When the booster balloons deflated and the rubber band loosened so that the middle balloon took off, the Loony Balloonies whooped and hollered happily. Soon the middle balloon was out of air and began wafting down to earth, but the little kite attached to it slowed its descent so that it swooped and spiraled in a gentle drift, finally landing in the grass with a whisper. Wayne ran to pick it up off the ground and held it above his head, and the whole crowd cheered loudly. Maryellen noticed with satisfaction that the Launchmen clapped, even Skip, though he clapped in slow motion.

The Loony Balloonies did not win the contest; a team from another school won with a three-foot-long rocket powered by gasoline. But the crowd cheered again, even louder than the first time, when Mr. Hagopian announced, "The judges have decided to award a special prize for creativity to . . ." He paused, then turned and beamed at Maryellen's team, "the Loony Balloonies!"

Maryellen was so surprised that she just stood there with her mouth open while the Karens and Angela hugged her with such force that, if she had been a balloon, she would have popped. Davy hollered, "Hurray!" And Wayne did cartwheels, which made the crowd cheer even longer.

"Nice job!" said Mr. Hagopian, congratulating Maryellen's team after the applause ended.

"Thanks," said Maryellen, still a bit stunned. "I didn't even know there was a prize for creativity."

"There wasn't," smiled Mr. Hagopian, looking even more pink and bald and shiny than usual. "We made it up on the spot, just for your team, because we thought you were so clever to have a machine with several stages. And we were impressed with the creative way you used simple materials to construct your machine."

"It was all stuff left over from my sister Joan's wedding," said Maryellen.

"But it took real creativity to figure out how to put it all together to make a flying machine," said Mr. Hagopian.

Some reporters and photographers came over to interview Mr. Hagopian. Maryellen and her team stood quietly watching as a TV reporter asked Mr. Hagopian questions and then held a microphone up to his mouth as he answered, while a TV camera whirred, filming it all.

When they had finished interviewing Mr. Hagopian, one of the newspaper photographers said to Maryellen, "Hey, I remember you. Aren't you the girl I photographed last May in the Memorial Day parade, riding in the car with the mayor?"

"Yes," said Maryellen. Suddenly, she was aware that

the TV camera was pointed toward her, and the TV reporter was holding his microphone up to catch what she said.

"What's your name, miss?" asked the TV reporter. "And why were you in the parade?"

Maryellen hesitated shyly.

"She's Maryellen Larkin!" said Karen Stohlman.

"She was in the parade because she put on a show to raise money for the March of Dimes to fight polio," added Karen King.

"All of us were stars in the show," said Wayne, mugging for the camera, "but mostly me."

"Why are you all here today?" asked the TV reporter.

Davy spoke up. "We entered the flying-machine contest," he said. "Thanks to Ellie, we won a special prize for creativity."

"And if there had been a prize for having the most fun, we'd have won that, too!" said Angela. All the Loony Balloonies murmured in happy agreement.

"So, Miss Maryellen Larkin," said the TV reporter. "You are a girl with good ideas for flying machines and for helping people. What is the most important idea you learned from this contest?" He pointed his microphone right at Maryellen, so she had to answer all alone.

She thought for a moment. "Well, you know, our flying machine was made up of ordinary things like balloons and rubber bands—not the kind of things you might expect a flying machine to be made of," she said. "But every part was equally important. Every part had its own job to do to make the machine fly." She grinned. "And it was the same with the Loony Balloonies. Our team was made up of different people who are good at different things. But every person was equally important, because to make the machine fly, we needed all those different things. It wouldn't have worked if we hadn't included everybody."

Maryellen paused and as she did, she looked at good old Davy, her funny, faithful friends the Karens and Angela, and zany Wayne. Then she went on, "I guess what I learned is that different is good. Just because an idea isn't what people expect, you still shouldn't ignore it. In fact, the best ideas come when you're *not* trying to be like everybody else."

"Ah," said the reporter. "I see. What you're saying

is that each one of us is an individual, and we contribute our unique abilities to the benefit of the group as a whole. So the most important thing that a team needs to do to succeed is—?"

"Listen," said Maryellen immediately. "Listen to each other. Because every idea deserves respect, and every person does, too."

✳

That evening, all the Larkins were in the living room watching TV when the local news came on. Everyone cheered and then shushed one another when the segment about the science contest began. First the TV reporter interviewed the winners of the contest, and they explained how their rocket worked. Then Mr. Hagopian came on, talking about how essential it was for American children to be competitive in science with children from other countries. Then the TV reporter said, "Now I'd like you to meet a fifth-grade girl who stands out—and is outstanding. Miss Maryellen Larkin."

And there was Maryellen, on TV, right in her own living room and in living rooms all over Florida.

As Maryellen, surrounded by her family, watched herself on TV surrounded by her friends—the Karens, Angela, Davy, and Wayne—she could hardly believe that what she was seeing was real. How long had she dreamed of this—being on television? But as she watched, Maryellen realized that this was even better than what she had dreamed of for so long. Because the great thing was that she was on TV as herself. She wasn't an imaginary character in an imaginary episode of an imaginary adventure. She wasn't a cowgirl galloping across the range, or a pioneer helping Davy Crockett. She was her own true, regular old self. In fact, that was *why* she was on TV, because she was who she was: the one and only Maryellen Larkin.

INSIDE Maryellen's World

Maryellen's idea to do a polio show for her birthday might seem odd today, but in 1954, polio was a big deal. Families feared polio almost as much as the atomic bomb. The disease, which usually struck children, often started like the flu, with a fever, aches, and weakness, but it could last many months and could cripple or even kill the patient. There was no cure, so patients were kept in isolation wards, away from their families, until they recovered. No wonder Maryellen remembered her illness as a dark, frightening time. When the vaccine was announced to be safe and effective, people wept with joy as church bells rang and car horns honked in celebration.

Still, some parents feared that the vaccine, which put a form of the virus into a person's body, might make their children sick. So doctors and health organizations worked to promote the vaccine, with great success. Since 1980, the United States has been polio free.

The 1950s brought other big scientific advances that changed the world. In fall 1955, when Maryellen's flying-machine contest takes place, the U.S. government began a project to launch a man-made satellite into orbit. When Russia launched its own rocket, *Sputnik*, first, America began pouring money into the "space race." In 1958, a small solar-powered satellite, *Vanguard 1*, was finally launched from Cape Canaveral, Florida. Today it's the oldest man-made satellite still orbiting the earth!

Along with new discoveries in science and medicine, Americans were also discovering their country. With the booming economy, more Americans than ever before had cars—and paid vacations. Popular TV shows like *Davy Crockett* and *The Lone Ranger* made many families want to see the real "Wild West," so they began taking long car trips, often to Yellowstone and other western parks.

Advances in health care and a strong economy made the 1950s a good time to be a kid—especially if you were in a middle-class white family. If you were a member of a minority, life was more difficult. In the South, where the Larkins lived, African Americans were *segregated*, or kept separate from, white Americans. It was harder for black families to travel, because many hotels and restaurants refused to serve them. Black children went to schools that were supposed to be "separate but equal"—but the reality was that the black schools had less money and sometimes not enough books or desks for their students. Linda Brown, an eight-year-old African American girl growing up in a racially mixed community in Topeka, Kansas, tried to enroll in the neighborhood school with her white friends, but the school board sent her to a black school farther away. So her father sued. The case, *Brown v. Board of Education*, went to the Supreme Court, which held that segregation was harmful and unconstitutional and must end. This decision became a landmark in the civil rights movement, which gained momentum during the 1950s and would bring even bigger changes in the decades to come.

Read more of MARYELLEN'S stories,

available from booksellers and at *americangirl.com*

✻ *Classics* ✻

Maryellen's classic series, now in two volumes:

Volume 1:
The One and Only

Maryellen wants to stand out—
but when she draws a cartoon of
her teacher, she also draws
unwanted attention. Still, her
drawing skills help her make a
new friend—with a girl her old
friends think of as an enemy!

Volume 2:
Taking Off

Maryellen's birthday party is a
huge hit! Excited by her fame,
she enters a science contest. But
can Maryellen invent a flying
machine *and* get her sister's
wedding off the ground?

✻ *Journey in Time* ✻

Travel back in time—and spend a few days with Maryellen!

The Sky's the Limit

Step into Maryellen's world of the 1950s! Go to a sock hop, or take
a road trip with the Larkin family all the way to Washington, D.C.
Choose your own path through this multiple-ending story.

✳ A Sneak Peek at ✳

The Sky's the Limit

My Journey with Maryellen

Meet Maryellen and take a journey back in time in a book that lets *you* decide what happens.

✳✳✳✳✳✳✳

Flying, that's what it feels like. My skis skim across the top of the snow so smoothly it's as if I'm a bird swooping low over the ground. I'm all by myself, with blue sky above, white snow below, and me in the middle, flying down the mountain, as fast as a shooting star.

I'm not skiing for fun; I'm skiing to win a race, and skiing to win is very, very serious. I'd love to go where I want to go, choosing whichever trail looks freshest and fastest and most fun. But I have to stick strictly to the planned race route and follow it exactly as it is marked and try to ski perfectly to win for my team.

It wasn't my idea to be on the ski team and turn skiing into something tense and competitive. It was my twin sister Emma's idea. She loves to compete. She especially loves to win. And she just about always wins when the two of us disagree. Emma is not only my twin sister, she is my best friend, and I always want to make her happy. That's how I ended up on the ski team. Emma really, really wanted us to do it together, so I gave in, as I usually do when Emma has her heart set on anything.

A sudden burst of wind makes the powdery snow

swirl up all around me. The sun reflecting off the snow blinds me just as the trail breaks into two narrow branches. I squint, looking for a route marker—a flag or an arrow—pointing to the branch that I should take. But if there is a marker, it's hidden by the whirling snow. Just then, someone waves, as if signaling me toward the left branch, so I take it. This branch of the trail winds through dense woods. Then, as I burst out into the open, it sends me over a huge mogul and I am airborne. That's fine with me. I love jumps—the higher, the better! But it's risky and unusual for a race route.

I zoom down the mountain, cross the finish line, and pass the time clock, and—to my amazement—I win the race.

I'm happy, though not as crazy excited as Emma would be. Winning means more to her than it does to me. I take off my gloves, skis, and goggles, and change my boots. I put on my eyeglasses and look for Emma as I hurry to the ski-race awards platform.

"Good job, Sophie! Way to go!" cheer my teammates. They gather around me and thump me on the back. Even Coach Stanislav is smiling for a change. In the crowd on the platform I see my proud parents and my grandmother. But where is Emma?

"Congratulations, Sophie," says the judge. She shakes my hand and gives me my prize.

"Whoa," I breathe. "Thanks." The prize is a fabulous vintage watch that's also a stopwatch. I take the beautiful watch out of its box, and I'm just strapping it onto my wrist when Emma appears.

"Sophie cheated," she says.

What?

"She took a shortcut," says Emma. "That's why she won."

"Emma!" I gasp. I plummet from happiness to humiliation in one second. How could she think that I would cheat? She's my sister, my other half, my twin. I know things have been a bit tense between us ever since our grandmother came to live with us and we've had to share a room. But is Emma so mad that she'd lie about me? Does she really think I cheated? I try to read Emma's face, but she won't meet my eyes.

✳

I'm not quick with words the way Emma is, and now I struggle to explain. "I must have—I think I made a mistake," I sputter. "I was blinded by the sun, and I couldn't see any flag, and I thought someone pointed me down the trail, and—"

"Sophie!" Coach Stanislav interrupts. I'm not surprised; even to my own ears, my explanation sounds weak. "If you cheated," my coach continues, "just be honest about it."

"I *didn't* cheat," I insist. "I'd *never* cheat. It was an honest mistake."

My mom slips her arm around my shoulders to comfort me.

"We'll have to look into what happened, Coach," says the judge. She turns to me and holds out her hand for the watch.

I undo the wrist strap with trembling, clumsy fingers. By mistake I touch the stopwatch button, and—*swoosh!*

Just for a second—

Just for the blink of an eye—

Just like when I was skiing—I have the sensation of flying, like a shooting star. And when it stops, I find myself . . . well, I'm not sure *where* I am.

I'm no longer on the ski mountain, that's for sure.

Instead, I'm standing on a driveway by a small house. There's a station wagon in the driveway, along with a big silver camper trailer. A hot sun reflects off the trailer, and I realize that I'm roasting in my ski-team uniform.

The air is moist, and it smells nice, all fruity and flowery. The driveway is bordered with palm trees, flowers, and large bushes heavy with—*lemons*? I touch one. Yup, it's a lemon.

Where am I? What has happened to me? It's obvious that I'm not in my snow-dusted hometown of Cedar Top, North Carolina, anymore.

I look at the watch, still in my hand. The last thing I did was accidentally press the stopwatch button. Could it possibly be the *watch* that transported me? If I press the button again, will it transport me home?

My heart quickens with hope. Maybe the watch will take me back to the moment on the trail before I chose the wrong route, before Emma's betrayal—before any of the bad stuff had happened yet.

But maybe the watch will transport me somewhere else entirely. Then what?

There's only one way to find out.

I touch the watch button, and . . .

Swoosh! . . . Once again, I feel as if I'm flying . . .

When I open my eyes, I'm back on the awards platform at the ski slope. Mom has her arm around me. Dad and Gran look sad. Coach Stanislav and the judge are frowning at me, and I can practically feel the chill waves of disapproval from all my teammates. It's as if *no time at all* has passed, as if no one has so much as taken a breath.

If only I could prove that I did not cheat, that I just made a mistake. But how? Emma, who usually leads the way and often speaks for me, is my *accuser.*

I feel lost, hopeless, and overwhelmed. Suddenly, I just want to disappear.

Will the watch transport me again? I'd like to go back to the warm place, but I'd rather go *anywhere* than stay here. I love the stars, the moon, and the planets—I'd gladly go to another planet right now!

No one will miss me; they are frozen in the moment. And I need some time to figure out what to do about the ski race.

So, mustering all my bravery, I close my eyes and press the stopwatch button again.

✻

Swoosh . . .

I'm swept up in the flying sensation . . . and when I open my eyes, I'm back on the driveway, next to the lemon bushes. I feel a warm rush of relief to be back in this balmy, palmy place.

I'm admiring the camper trailer—it's as stream-lined and silvery as a rocket ship—when the side door of the house opens and a girl about my age comes out.

She's skinny and cheerful-looking. Her reddish-gold hair is in a bouncy ponytail that catches the sun-shine. A roly-poly dachshund waddles behind her as well as two cute little boys—one is wearing a fireman's hat—and a little girl wearing a tutu and a cardboard crown.

I freeze, expecting suspicious questions about who I am and what I'm doing in their driveway.

Instead, the ponytail girl smiles a friendly smile and says, "Oh, hi! I'm Maryellen Larkin! Don't you just love the Airstream trailer? Everybody does. By the way, this is my sister Beverly. She's seven. The fireman is Tom, he's five, and the littlest guy is

Mikey, who's three. Our dog is Scooter. We're so glad you're here!"

The littlest boy, Mikey, runs forward and flings his arms around my legs, practically knocking my eyeglasses off in the exuberance of his welcome.

Maryellen rattles on. "We've been excited ever since we heard that you were coming. You're going to love Daytona Beach."

Daytona Beach? Isn't that in Florida? I'm in *Florida*? And Maryellen and her family have been *expecting* me? I'm so flabbergasted that I'm breathless.

Tom, the boy in the fireman hat, asks, "What's your name?"

"Sophie," I manage to choke out.

I don't know why, but my name makes all the Larkins smile. I've never thought of my name or myself as a reason to smile before. It feels good, I discover. I begin to relax a little.

"Sophie?" says Maryellen merrily. "Are you named after the singer Sophie Tucker? We see her on *The Ed Sullivan Show* a lot."

I shrug and grin. "I don't know," I say. I've never heard of Sophie Tucker or *The Ed Sullivan Show*. "Mom told me my grandmother thought up my name."

"My grandpop gave me the nickname Ellie," says Maryellen. Then she asks, "How old are you?"

"Ten," I answer.

"Me too!" says Maryellen.

"Do you have any brothers or sisters?" asks Beverly-with-the-crown.

I nod. "A sister," I say, tensing up a bit when I think of Emma.

"Mom's excited to meet you," says Maryellen. "Your Aunt Betty is one of her oldest friends."

"Betty visited us last year," Beverly cuts in.

"It was Mom's idea for you to come stay with us while Betty helps your parents move from New York to Washington, D.C." Maryellen starts to lead me toward the house. "It's lucky that Betty works for the airlines, so your ticket was free. Let's go inside. Mom can call your parents and tell them you're here."

"Uh . . ." I begin. I'm so confused and not sure what to say.

Just as Maryellen starts to open the screen door, Beverly stops her.

"Wait, Ellie," she says. "How do you know that

Sophie is Betty's niece? Maybe she's a new girl who's moving into the neighborhood." Beverly turns to me and tilts her head. "Is that it?" she asks. "Are you and your family moving in?"

✳ *To go inside with Maryellen,*
   turn to page 15.

✳ *To agree with Beverly,*
   turn to page 17.

About the Author

VALERIE TRIPP says that she became a writer because of the kind of person she is. She says she's curious, and writing requires you to be interested in everything. Talking is her favorite sport, and writing is a way of talking on paper. She's a daydreamer, which helps her come up with her ideas. And she loves words. She even loves the struggle to come up with just the right words as she writes and rewrites. Ms. Tripp lives in Maryland with her husband.

✻✲✻